THE AUSTRALIAN CLASSICS LIBRARY

Tales of the Austral Tropics

Ernest Favenc

Introduction by Cheryl Taylor

General editors

Bruce Bennett, University of New South Wales

Robert Dixon, University of Sydney

SYDNEY UNIVERSITY PRESS

Published 2009 by Sydney University Press
SYDNEY UNIVERSITY PRESS
Fisher Library, University of Sydney
www.sup.usyd.edu.au

First published in 1894 by Osgood, McIlvaine and Co., London

This, the Australian Classics Library text of *Tales of the Austral Tropics* is a repaging of text files on SETIS, themselves input from the 1894 edition published by Osgood, McIlvaine and Co., London

© Introduction by Cheryl Taylor 2009
© Sydney University Press 2009

The publication of this book is part of the University of Sydney Library's Australian Studies electronic texts initiative. Further details are available at www.sup.usyd.edu.au/oztexts/

Front cover image: portrait of Ernest Favenc (by L.W. Appleby). Courtesy of the Mitchell Library, State Library of NSW

ISBN 978-1-920898-99-1

Contents

Introduction

After he arrived from England in 1863, aged eighteen, Ernest Favenc's adventures in Australia took the classic forms of jackerooing, droving, exploring, and prospecting. These provided the subject matter for writing, and between 1871 and his death in 1908 Favenc published nine serials and nearly 100 short stories in Queensland and New South Wales newspapers, as well as poems, novels for children, and a centennial *History of Australian Exploration* (1888). Stories printed in the Sydney *Bulletin* in the 1890s, some of which Favenc re-edited for volume publication, earned him a place in Australian literary history.

The Last of Six (1893) was the third in the *Bulletin* series of story and verse anthologies. The volume's bush themes, heightened by the supernatural and the sensational, epitomise the story-telling fashions that prevailed before Henry Lawson, who found his voice as a fiction writer in eighteen *Bulletin* stories published that year (Hadgraft, Introduction). However Favenc's subtitle, *Tales of the Austral Tropics*, retained as the title for a revised selection printed in London in 1894, pinpoints his stories' distinguishing feature. Their tropical settings exclude such southern Australian subjects as bushrangers and the convict system, as well as themes popularised by Lawson, such as the Sydney-bush dichotomy. Favenc assumes rather than dwells on male camaraderie (mateship), but bushmen's rivalry and enmity are his frequent subjects. In such morally charged tales as 'That Other Fellow', his concern is with Dickensian heroic and redemptive friendship. Favenc approaches the tropical coastal and inland landscapes from an explorer's viewpoint, as picturesque but menacing obstacles. Deserts decide the characters' fates in many of his stories.

Most of Favenc's stories also privilege Anglo-Saxon or Anglo-Celtic gentlemanliness and bushcraft as rational norms that invite identification. From this perspective the plots expose deficiencies in women and other races or nationalities. In the opening story, 'The Last of Six', the compassionate bushmen and the distraught, tragic Frenchwoman establish this opposition. A second premise is the capitalist tenet that ownership of land or property confers status and determines social levels. Beyond these assumptions, *The Last of Six* testifies to anxieties that underlay and helped to shape the embryonic national identity. These concerned wealth as a motive for colonisation and the colonisers' relationships with Aborigines.

By representing gold and jewels as sources of corruption leading to death, Favenc's stories impose ethical limits on the drive that motivated settlement. Condemnations of greed are less common today than they were in nineteenth- and early-twentieth-century texts, but Favenc is unusually persistent in shaping his plots into validations of the Biblical text that defines the love of money as the root of all evil (1 Timothy 6.10). Examples are the trove of rubies that sets in motion the calamitous events of 'A Haunt of the Jinkarras', the gold reef in 'Spirit-Led', and the illusory diamond mines and alluvial gold in 'The Spell of the Mas-Hantoo'. Above all, 'The Story of a Big Pearl' traces a series of crimes and supernatural punishments emanating from a luminous jewel. The version in *The Last of Six* abridges the original *Bulletin* story, apparently with a view to restricting the deaths suffered by the pearl's corrupt possessors to non-European races, and to removing references to the recent *Quetta* shipwreck disaster (Taylor *xxx* and 35–50).

An article that Favenc contributed to the *Sydney Mail* in September 1882, in which he refutes charges of 'atrocities' brought against northern settlers by southern newspapers, is a key to his attitude to Aborigines. In reporting his Northern Territory exploration in the *Mail* a year later, Favenc refers innocuously to Aboriginal cultural practices, but the expedition diary of Emily Caroline Creaghe testifies at first hand to such 'atrocities' as he denies. At Lawn Hill station, the manager, Jack Watson, had forty pairs of ears nailed around the walls, collected during reprisals against Aborigines for cattle stealing. Stockmen brought Bella, 'a new wild gin', to the station 'by the usual method'—dragged along from horseback by a rope around the neck—and chained her to a tree in pouring rain until she should become 'tamed' (Monteath 26, 29). Thus Favenc reinforced the silence that concealed violence against Aborigines.

Parallel repressions occur in his stories, where, however, the representation of Aborigines is more complex. In 'A Cup of Cold Water', 'A Lucky Meeting' and 'That Other Fellow', Aboriginal characters perform essential services in marginal positions as whites' subordinates. They fit invisibly into these narratives because they act out their naturalised roles in colonial societies and texts. However Favenc's references to Aborigines elsewhere suggest either guilt, or fear of Indigenous cultures as an unknowable 'other'.

Some references dissociate ordinary settlers from responsibility for abuses, in accordance with Favenc's disclaimer in the *Mail*. In 'Spirit-Led', which echoes the *Bulletin*'s anti-clericalism, guilt shifts to the maniacal drunkard Delaine, a clergyman's son haunted by an Aboriginal slain during a Tableland 'dispersal'. The criminal 'ghost' finally hanged in 'The Cook and the Cattle-Stealer' claims to have been present at Murderer's Camp, 'where all the niggers were shot one Christmas day'. Finally, 'Malchook's Doom' contrasts the non-white or cowardly perpetrators of torture, murder and rape with the decent stockmen whose spokesman is the first-person narrator.

Favenc's advocacy for northern settlers' behaviour towards Aborigines emerges again in other stories that deal centrally with inter-racial relations. In 'The Missing Super', a newcomer's choice of flogging as a punishment motivates a poetic revenge. Favenc evinces sympathy for the avenger Powlang, but 'dispersals' reinstate white supremacy in the story's conclusion. 'Tranter's Shot' undermines the credence given by outsiders to settlers' 'murderous treatment of the natives' by substituting a non-human as the victim of a shooting by 'an old Gulf hand'. Favenc's most anthologised story, 'The Parson's Blackboy', dismisses clerical qualms about white men's cohabitation with Aboriginal women on the basis that this was a 'custom of the country'. By contrast, 'Pompey', which tells of a tragedy stemming from such a liaison, is a rarity among colonial texts because it raises a major repressed anxiety, namely white fathers' feelings for their abandoned Aboriginal children.

Favenc's stories sometimes express contempt for Aboriginal people, for example by associations with dogs and by a standardised censuring of eating and sleeping habits. While 'Pompey', 'Malchook's Doom' and 'The Missing Super', draw on Aboriginal warrior culture in order to sanitise white violence as retaliatory, some passages satirise the tribesmen's powers of resistance, presumably in an effort to soothe the pioneers' actual fears of attack. Examples are the mock-heroic description that opens 'The Mystery of Baines' Dog', and a sardonic reference to Pompey's departure for 'the happy hunting ground'.

In other stories, however, marginal references endow Aboriginal people with a mysterious power. In 'A Cup of Cold Water', the dying Manning scrawls his name and the date on a rock, amongst 'rude markings, the work of aborigines … the trails of serpents and lizards, and … the mystic footprint of the aboriginal devil'. This reads like a last attempt to overwrite the unfamiliar. Again, in 'Spirit-Led' bushmen attribute to 'blacks' the wild cries, 'arising out of the surrounding solitude', that presage the sudden supernatural transformation of a living man to a skeleton. In the colonial imagination, therefore, Indigenous people remain as presences in the seemingly empty bush.

'A Haunt of the Jinkarras' uses narrative devices popularised by Edgar Allen Poe to evoke even more intensely settlers' fears of the unknown. The pitch-black of the cave into which Jackson vanishes and the waters that trap the narrator evoke the opaqueness of Indigenous cultures to European powers of perception. More realistically, the blackness of the cave and the distorted shapes of the Jinkarras, associated under the Manichean fallacy with dirt and stink, invite interpretation as a projection of the colonisers' stereotyped disparagement of Aborigines. Identified with the 'missing link' of the popular Darwinian science of the day, the

Jinkarras are, for the modern reader, the most troubling expression of Favenc's racial contempt. Just as Manning asserted European identity by inscribing numbers and letters among the symbols of Australian nature and Aboriginal spirituality, so the narrator survives by holding firmly to reason as he counts the hours. His emergence into 'the blessed glorious light' promises the ultimate triumph of European 'rational' civilisation over the Indigenous darkness unconsciously dreaded by Favenc's bushman narrators.

The story-telling methods of *The Last of Six* are unfashionable now. Characters' feelings and motives lack subtlety, and the reader can feel the machinery as it grinds out the over-neat or clever plots. Narrative twists that produced superstitious shivers or religious gratification a century ago have little power over present-day readers. *The Last of Six* nevertheless holds lasting cultural value for Australians, because it exemplifies the assumptions and anxieties of the first generation of settlers in the country's north.

Cheryl Taylor
James Cook University

References

Favenc, Ernest. 'Diary of a Trip from North Newcastle to Macarthur River.' *Sydney Mail*, 10 November 1883, 879; 24 November, 969–70; 1 December, 1014; 8 December, 1072; 15 December, 1113; 22 December, 1160.

Favenc, Ernest. 'White versus Black.' *Sydney Mail*, 30 September 1882, 544.

Hadgraft, Cecil. *The Australian Short Story before Lawson*. Melbourne: Oxford University Press, 1986.

Monteath, Peter, ed. *The Diary of Emily Caroline Creaghe Explorer*. North Adelaide: Corkwood Press, 2004.

Taylor, Cheryl, ed. *Ernest Favenc: Tales of the Austral Tropics*. Sydney: UNSW Press, 1997.

TALES OF THE AUSTRAL TROPICS

BY

ERNEST FAVENC

LONDON

OSGOOD, McILVAINE & CO.

45 ALBEMARLE STREET, W.

1894

[Facsimile of first edition titlepage]

PREFACE

IN these 'Tales of the Austral Tropics' will be found the strange romances which write themselves, often in letters of blood, amid the half-unknown, mysterious regions of Tropical Australia. That they are not less true than terrible, I take it upon myself to affirm. That such is far from being the case with the larger proportion of literary manufacture professing to describe Australian life and character, I most distinctly assert. 'Those who know seldom write, and those who write don't know,' remarks the veteran colonist with accentuated emphasis. But this author's name is a household word among bushmen and bookmen from Albany to Thursday Island, from 'The Gulf' to the Snowy River—

> Alike to him the sea, the shore,
>
> The pen, the bridle, and the oar.

To him, familiar as highways are the endless solitudes of the 'Never Never Country'—he has tempted the Desert Sphinx, gazed upon gold matrix and opal hoards which gleamed in mockery of the exhausted wanderer. Trusted for dear life in forest glades to a steady eye and a true rifle. Listened in a canoe on the Coral Sea to the moaning of the approaching tempest.

Long a leading actor upon Dame Nature's stage, he has turned scene-painter for the nonce, and limned with lifelike effect the drama of the Waste.

ROLF BOLDREWOOD.

A CUP OF COLD WATER

A SILENT and gloomy man. For a man of wealth, who, at one time, had been noted for his social qualities and his hospitality, Marten was looked upon with some little wonder by those who lived in his neighbourhood. People spoke of his solitary habits and the frightened, hunted look he always had in his eyes. Rumour even said that that stalwart and attentive man-servant of his was, in reality, a keeper.

Marten was a man whom vengeance had overtaken in this world and he could never forget it.

*   *   *

Dull, dark scrub all around, a sandy, barren soil underfoot, a cloudless sky and a hot, relentless sun overhead. Even more desolate than the usual dreary-looking scrub of the interior of Australia is this lonely thicket. The trunks of the stunted trees are gnarled and crooked, the foliage is scant and almost shadeless, the ground absolutely free from all undergrowth, and a deep, lifeless quiet reigns throughout. Footsteps and laboured breathing; and the repose of the scene is broken by the appearance of a human figure, a worn and wearied man slowly and painfully dragging himself along some horse-tracks forming a trail through the scrub. The unfortunate traveller is a pitiable sight, his sun-scorched face is thin and haggard with starvation, and his bloodshot eyes gleam with the delirium of thirst, his boots are absolutely ragged, and he leaves a bloody track on the baked ground. At times he sinks beneath the mockery of shade thrown by one of the scrub-trees, then, after a brief rest, renews his toilsome way.

Presently a break is visible ahead, and with restored hope the exhausted man pushes on, and ere long, with a hoarse, inarticulate cry of joy, emerges from the scrub on to the bank of a river. A river such as had haunted his dreams—clear, bright, sparkling, splashing in tiny rivulets amongst granite boulders, and rippling from one wide pool to another.

But the river has a strange appearance—no trees line its banks, no rushes fringe its shore, the bed is like a broad channel cut through the sandy waste around; down the centre runs the stream of water, the sight of which has brought fresh life to the worn-out wanderer. Slowly he toils across the hot and heavy sand to one of the shallow pools that sparkle in the sunlight, flings himself down and plunges his burning face and cracked lips into the crystal stream, then raises his head quickly with a bitter cry of pain—for this delusive, mocking river is saltier than the sea.

The first moments of despair passed, the traveller gathers himself together again for a struggle to the last, retraces his steps to the bank and searches for the continuation of the horse-tracks he has been following. Finding these, he once more plunges into the sea of scrub that lines either bank of the river, and slowly staggers on. Three hours have passed and the sun is getting low when there is again a break in the weary, monotonous thicket—a small, comparatively clear patch of country, in the centre of which rises a conical hill of bare granite rock, lifting its bald crest and smooth, glistening sides nearly a hundred feet above the expanse of sad-coloured tree-tops. The open space encircling the foot of the rock is covered with short grass, there are several clumps of cork-trees scattered about, and in a deep depression at the base of the hill is one of the rock-holes peculiar to Western Australia, nearly half full of rain-water—a deep hole almost like a tank hollowed out by human hands.

Refreshed by a long drink, the man eagerly surveys the signs of a late encampment. He thrusts his hand into the ashes of the fire, but they are cold. He searches anxiously for any scraps of food that may have been left behind, but without avail. Then another hope comes to him, and with his last remaining strength he climbs the side of the naked rock and stands upright on the summit gazing around,

A terribly depressing panorama meets his view, lit up by the last rays of the declining sun. North, south and east is a grim, black expanse of scrub without opening, save that here and there he can recognise the sheen of the treacherous saltwater river. As far as eye can see stretches this lonely, lifeless waste, that owns no boundary save the blue haze of the horizon. He then turns to the west. The same stern uniformity, the only difference being that a dark-blue, square-topped range is visible far off. No smoke arises anywhere, neither break nor clearing is visible; all is silent, merciless and dead. With one last, despairing look he recognises that the great wilderness has pronounced his doom, and, with hopeless step, descends to the rocky hole and throws himself down to await the coming of his last and only friend.

Darkness sets in; the clear stars shine bright in a moonless sky, one by one the southern constellations sink lower and lower until they are swallowed up in the black shadow of the gloomy scrub. The distant whoop of an owl, or the melancholy wail of some other night-bird alone breaks the oppressive stillness, but the sleeper heeds them not. Nature has been kind to him at last and brought him painless slumber. In pleasant dreams his mind wanders far away from the foot of the giant rock where his body rests. The grey dawn finds him still alive, but the bitterness of death has passed, he neither cares nor thinks of rescue or relief; the encircling desert has lost its terrors, he is half-way to another world. Still there is something to be done, and he takes a loose bit of stone, and drags himself alongside a flat rock which is covered with rude markings, the work of the aborigines: imitations of the tracks of kangaroos and emus, the trails of serpents and lizards, and, keeping guard over all, a gigantic human track with six toes, the mystic footprint of the aboriginal devil.

Amongst these savage emblems the dying man scrawls his name and the date; that done, he feels that his earthly cares are over. He thrusts his hand inside his shirt as though to grasp some object there with loving care, and with a sigh of relief his head falls back and he thinks no more of heat or thirst or hunger, for Death, the comforter, has brought him full release.

*   *   *

Four months have passed, the weather has been unchanged. Day after day a cloudless sun has looked down on the lonely body, gradually shrivelling up into a withered mummy: day after day has seen it untouched by bird or beast; even the scavenger crows have shunned the spot, and the dead white man has lain in solitude all the time. Two men are now standing by the remains, horses are feeding around on the dry grass, and two black boys are kindling a fire a short distance away. One of the men, a young fellow of about three-and-twenty, kneels down and reverently takes from the fleshless hand the object it has held so long in the clutch of death—a worn and weather-stained note-book. Rising, he calls to one of the blacks to bring a blanket, which he throws over the body, and the two go silently to their camp.

'Tom,' says the young man, 'we have found what we started to look for sooner than I expected. God help Marten when I meet him!'

'The black boy's yarn must have been right,' returned Tom.

'True as Gospel. Over a hundred and fifty miles he must have come in on foot, starving, and for every mile my father trod to meet his death here on this rock, the murdering cur who left him out there to die shall suffer bitterly in return, or my name's not Manning. Now, let us see what he has written.'

The message of the dead man to his son was short, but pregnant. It ran:—

> While I was away from camp Marten packed up, and taking all the horses and the two boys, started home. I came back with my horse knocked up and sore-footed and found the camp deserted. We discovered some splendid country on the heads of the G— and the L—, and I think he means to go down and take it up for himself, trusting to my never turning up again. I must follow on foot as best I can, for my horse is dead lame … I have been walking now for two days and my feet are cut to pieces on the ranges; perhaps when I get down on the level country I may get along better … Quite knocked up; I have done my best but can hold out no longer; if anyone finds this let them take it and the note to my son, John Manning, Ballarat, Victoria.

Between the leaves was one, torn out and folded note-shape. It ran:

> DEAR JACK,—Marten left me to die of starvation at the head of
> the L— River. I have struggled along so far, but must lie down and
> die here. God bless you, my boy.

There was silence after reading this. Tom broke it first.

'Marten sold the country well, didn't he?'

'Yes, almost immediately he got back, there was a bit of a craze for
country just then.'

'But for that nigger we'd never have dropped on the rights of it.'

'No, Marten supposed that the two boys would go back to their country—
never dreamt that I would come over here on a forlorn hope of finding
my father and run across one of them. He said, too, that he found the
good country after my father was lost, so that I had no share in the
proceeds of the sale.'

'Shall we bury him now?' said Tom at last, after a pause.

Young Manning nodded, and they proceeded with their task. By sundown
the long-neglected body, that had lain unwatched on the desolate rock,
was consigned to the earth, and, next morning, the son set himself the
labour of carving out in more permanent characters the name of the man
who rested there.

'Tom,' said Manning, when his work was done, 'I have made up my mind
how to act, and I want you to keep quiet about my father's death. I intend
giving that fellow rope enough and coming down on him when he least
expects it. It would be impossible to sheet this home to him by law, so I
shall use other means. I can trust you, I know.'

'About the boys?' returned Tom.

'We'll discharge them before we get back to town, and it's not likely
Marten will ever run against any of them again.'

In an hour's time the rock mound and the new-made grave were as lonely
as before.

*　　*　　*

James H. Marten, Esq., was a rich man, the few thousands he had made out of pastoral country in the western colony had been well invested in mining shares, and he had been one of the few who had made money by a mining-boom. He still dabbled in it, although there was no necessity for him doing so, but the fever was yet in his veins, and the fascination of a new reef had all its old attraction for him. At the present time he had, as he thought, 'a big thing on' in Kimberley[1]—he had just had a satisfactory interview with a man who showed him specimens 'rich enough to boom any company along until the bottom dropped out of it.' Marten had half a mind to go up north and look at it himself; he was getting too stout, he thought, and a good rough trip would set him up again—why, he'd been leading a sedentary life ever since that trip with Manning. And as the thought came back to him he picked up his hat and went out hastily, for he felt as though there was something strange locked up in the office with him.

Thus affected by nervous fears, due, as he thought, to inertia, Marten, after some hesitation, finally decided on the Kimberley trip, and, in company with the prospector who had brought him the specimens, whose name was Tom Howard, started for the North. The camp where the reef was situated was one of the furthest outlying ones, and by the time they reached it Marten felt that he was rapidly getting back to hard condition again. Nearly a week passed, and the mining magnate was quite satisfied that he had a most profitable speculation, whatever the public might find it in the end, when there was a new arrival in the camp—a friend of the prospector's, who had been on a long trip southward. After some mysterious conferences, Marten was taken into confidence and shown specimens that made his mouth water. The man who brought them into camp had found them nearly one hundred and fifty miles to the south-west; there was a patch of desert country to cross, but that was nothing with such a lure ahead. Marten, who now felt in his old bush form,

---

[1] Kimberley, in N.W. Australia.

consented to go with the stranger and look at the new find so that he could make a personal report in Melbourne, and they started.

Marten found his new companion taciturn and reserved; he would take his meals apart in solitary fashion, and sleep some distance off. Marten had seen the same moodiness before in men who had long lived an 'outside' life, and he thought nothing of it—the more stupid the man, the better for him. Strange schemes intruded themselves into his brain of playing his companion the trick he had played Manning, if the reef turned out anything like the specimens that had been produced. If Fortune dealt trumps in his hand why should he not take advantage of them? Their way was a weary one, some of it across sandy spinifex plains, and part of it through mulga—only twice did they come to any water, in each instance a brackish native well. On the fourth day they reached rough, broken country, and his companion pointed to a range and said that the reef was there. That night they camped at a small rock-hole which just sufficed for their wants and those of their horses. Next morning the prospector said they must leave their spare horses and ride on, look at the reef, and come back, as there was no water beyond this place.

After about three hours' ride they halted at the foot of a frowning range from which some deep ravines ran down into the lower country. Here the prospector pulled up. 'We had better,' he said, 'tie our horses to this tree and go up the gully on foot—it's too rough for horses.' They dismounted. 'I am not quite sure which of the two gullies it is—they are both so much alike; you go up this one and I'll go up the other. If you see anything of my old tracks fire your revolver; if not, come back here and wait for me.'

They parted, and Marten made an unsuccessful ascent of the gully. There were no tracks nor any signs of auriferous country, and tired, thirsty, and disgusted, he returned to the rendezvous.

The horses were gone! Was it possible he had made a mistake? No; there were the tracks. Had they broken their bridles and made off? A distant noise drew his attention to a ridge about half-a-mile away. There was the prospector riding homewards, leading Marten's horse. Marten yelled and 'coo-eed' without attracting any attention; then he drew his revolver to fire a shot, but an empty click was the only response. He looked at it; the cartridges had been removed. There was no doubt he was being purposely left behind. As this thought flashed through his mind, the receding man pulled up on the crest of the ridge and looked back. Taking off his hat, he waved a mocking salute, and then vanished down the far side.

With all the terror that now crowded into Marten's brain there was one predominant question—what was the motive for deserting him? Then a cold shiver ran through him. Had Manning come to life after all and paid someone to play him this trick? He rallied himself and started to follow the track of the horses. It was evident no one would come back for him; he must help himself. It was dark when he got to the rock-hole where they had camped the night before, and, although he knew that it could not be otherwise, yet it was with horror he noticed that the place was deserted, packs, horses, everything gone. There was a little muddy water at the bottom of the hole, and he drank it greedily. He passed an awful night, the mysterious suddenness of the blow overwhelmed him. If he had had a chance to argue or explain it would have been different, but all around him was silence and the desert. 'Plead to that!' a mocking voice seemed to say.

Next morning at grey dawn he was off along the back track, and doggedly pursued his way until the loose sand and spinifex compelled him to seek rest. He had no water-bag, so he had thrown his useless revolver away and filled the pouch with some of the muddy water, perhaps he could struggle through to the second native well—but 60 miles!—it was a long way. That night was passed in the slumber of exhaustion; next morning, with stiffened limbs, he recommenced his march, and now his watersupply was exhausted. Noontide found him lying under a mulga-bush, praying for death. The sound of an approaching horse aroused him; the prospector had repented and turned back. He halted near the exhausted man, and, leaning on his horse's neck looked calmly at him. 'Do you know who I am?' he said. 'I am Jack Manning, the son of the man you murdered. I have brought you out here to die the same death you condemned him to. I know everything, I found his dead body, his notebook, and a letter to me, I also found one of the boys you had with you. My father followed you nearly one hundred and fifty miles, then he died of hunger and exhaustion; I intend you to do the same, and also to have the pleasure of watching you do it. I have no intention of letting you die just yet, so I will give you a quart of water and you must make that do until you reach the second well.' Manning dismounted, filled his quart-pot from the water-bag he was carrying and placed it on the ground, when, just as he was riding off, the wretched man broke the spell of shameful silence that held him and begged and implored mercy. It was useless. As though stone-deaf, Manning rode away and left him to plead to the sand, the mulga, and the spinifex; once more the silence and horror of the desert were around him.

On the fourth day, in a state of delirium, he staggered to the native well and buried his face in the tepid, brackish water. His enemy was not visible. Should he wait here for death? He fell unconscious while thinking.

When he awoke it was morning, and he thought he would make the attempt to reach the other well; perhaps his foe would relent. He staggered wearily on, and when the day grew hot sank down at the foot of a sand-ridge.

'Do you repent?' said a voice. Manning was standing over him. His swollen tongue refused to answer, but he feebly raised his hand. 'Drink,' said his enemy: 'I cannot see even *you* die of thirst.'

With all the fierce longing burning within him for the sweet, cool draught, he yet thought that it were better to die now than live to undergo it all once more, and, with a last effort, he put the proffered bag aside. 'Let me die,' he groaned in a scarcely audible voice. 'Drink,' said the other, 'I will spare your life, though I cannot forgive; drink, and repent.'

He held the mouth of the bag to his enemy's lips and moistened them. The touch of the cool water was too much; with a feverish grasp the half-dead man seized the bag and drank greedily. Then, with a wild laugh, he fell back insensible.

'Is it too late, I wonder?' thought Manning, looking at him.

It was not too late for his life; but his reason never quite recovered. Ever since he has been haunted by the nightmare of that dreadful tramp through the waterless desert, with the avenger ever dogging his footsteps.

THE RUMFORD PLAINS TRAGEDY

I. Statement Made By Gilbert Vaughan, Manager of the L.S.D. Bank, Wattleville.

IT was a serious difficulty, and had occurred so suddenly that my presence of mind entirely forsook me—I saw no way out of it save instant flight. There lay the dead body, slain by my hand, and in a few moments I should be confronted with the girl whom I had intended to make my wife. How was I to face her, knowing how fondly she had loved the poor victim?

The act had been quite unintentional. Although there had never been much love lost between us, I had not meant his death. It had been simply the fault of hasty temper on my side and unfortunate curiosity on his. I had ridden out that day, my heart filled with the gentlest feelings; the bright morning and sunny landscape seemed to whisper naught but peace, and now, by an inconsiderate blow, I had dispelled all my hopes, and saw no escape but in prompt and immediate disappearance from the scene. To continue standing by the poor corpse would be the act of an idiot. By a strange chance no one was about; I had ridden up quite unperceived. So I mounted my horse and hastened back to the township which I had left that morning with such different feelings.

My duties at the bank that day (I was the manager of a small country branch) were, fortunately for me, of the slightest, for my mind was constantly running on the morning's tragedy, and I was ceaselessly wondering if my deed had been discovered, and picturing the sorrow of the innocent girl whom I so fondly loved. At three o'clock I heard a voice in the bank asking the teller if I was in, and soon afterwards, to my amazement, Ah Foo, the Chinese cook at Rumford Plains, walked into the small apartment that served as manager's room.

As he glanced at me with his cunning almond eyes I saw in a moment that my secret was known, and it did not need that he should take out two small objects and place them on the table to confirm this suspicion. For an instant I had wild thoughts of shooting him down with the bank revolver and swearing that he had tried to stick up the place, but I restrained myself in order to hear what he had to say.

'I saw you kill him, Misser Vawn, and I welly glad. No fear I say anyting. Evelybody ask. I no savee. Evelybody say Misser Muspius; I no savee, only laugh. Missee Lawrence she cly, cly, all day. Think it Misser Muspius doee.'

'Ah Foo,' I said, 'you're a brick; here's a sovereign for you.'

'Allight, Misser Vawn. I no savee who kill him, only, when evelybody say, Misser Muspius, I laugh—' and he laughed himself out of the room, only to reappear for an instant. 'You go, see Missee Lawrence to-night?' he whispered in a stage aside, and vanished.

Of course I would. I would make the most of the golden opportunity. Muspius, my hated rival, was evidently suspected, and Ah Foo had slyly confirmed these suspicions. I was safe, so long as I could bribe Ah Foo; at any rate, I would take his advice and go to Rumford Plains at once; it was only five miles, and I would arrange that the suspicions thrown on Muspius should be confirmed. I had taken the first step in crime; the second was easy.

II. Statement Made by John Muspius, Superintendent of Merridale Station.

It was a pure accident, but a most unfortunate one, to happen on the very morning when I rode over to Rumford Plains to propose to Miss Lawrence. Just as I was going to hang my horse up I saw Tommy standing at the low fence, with his head over the second rail, watching me. Now, I had had more than one bridle broken through his tricks, and after ineffectually telling him several times to clear out, I gave him a tap with the double of my whip. It caught him on the back of the neck, and, to my astonishment, he dropped down dead. It struck me at once that no one would believe it was an accident, for only the other evening I had got into a dispute with Lawrence about shooting blacks in North Queensland; and he had said that he would not trust anyone's life in my hands. Of course he was in a temper because I had the best of the argument, but this accident happening just after such a remark would look altogether too suspicious; and besides, I dared not face Miss Lawrence, for I knew how fond she was of Tommy. There was no one about, so I just rode quietly off into Wattleville to think it over.

About half-past two that afternoon old Jennings, landlord of the Royal, told me that Ah Foo, the cook at Rumford Plains, wanted to see me. 'Well, Ah Foo,' I said, when the old scoundrel came in, 'what do you want?' I had no suspicion at the time that he had witnessed the unhappy affair. He grinned and made a motion with his arm like striking a blow, which at once told me that he knew all. 'Welly unlucky, Misser Muspius,' he said, 'poor Tommy—dead.'

'Ah!' I said, 'it can't be helped. You know I never meant to kill him.'

'I savee,' he replied, 'I saw you. Evelyone say Misser Vawn kill Tommy. I no savee, only laugh. Missee Lawrence cly, cly, cly.' So that confounded bank jackeroo, Vaughan, was suspected, was he? Well, the best thing that could happen. I gave Ah Foo a sovereign, and he winked and said, 'You go see Missee Lawrence, I tink welly good.' Then he vanished. Under the circumstances this was excellent advice, and I determined to follow it. Of course I would not go out of my way to shift the blame on Vaughan, but if anything were said about the matter I would not hide my opinion of him. All's fair in love and war. Besides, he had no business to be out there at that time in the morning; serve him right if it proved the means of getting him into trouble.

III. Extract From the Diary of Miss Selina Lawrence.

May 1st—Such an unhappy commencement to the day; I never thought I should feel so glad afterwards as I do now. About 11 o'clock papa came to me to say that poor Tommy was dead—killed, seemingly, by a blow on the back of the neck! I almost fainted when I heard it. The men were all away at the yards, and no stranger had been seen about the place. Poor Tommy! I cried bitterly all the morning. His body was laid out and I put some flowers on it, he was such a good-hearted, faithful fellow. Papa is very indignant, and says he will never rest until the guilty party is found out; I never saw him so roused before. He says it is a most abominable crime to be committed in broad day. While I was still sorrowing over poor Tommy's fate the mail arrived. Such glorious news! A letter from Fred, saying that his uncle has retired and handed his practice over to him; so now there's no reason why we can't get married at once and bring our long engagement to an end—so he writes. Papa's very pleased, too; he said that the practice is worth nearly two thousand a year, and we are actually going to start for Sydney tomorrow morning, so I'm tired out packing up.

Mr. Vaughan and Mr. Muspius came over this evening. They both seemed very absent-minded and jealous of each other. I suppose Papa told them what had happened when they went out on the verandah to smoke, for they both, I am glad to say, went away early.

Poor Tommy! this good news put his death right out of my head for the moment.

IV. Statement of Ah Foo, Cook at Rumford Plains. (Translated into ordinary English.)

I remember May 1st. I was looking out of the kitchen window when I saw Mr. Vaughan ride up. Just as he approached the house, Tommy, Miss Lawrence's pet emu, went up and pecked at the buckles on his saddlepouch, and his horse started back and broke the bridle. Mr. Vaughan turned back and caught his horse, and when Tommy came up again, he hit him with the butt-end of his whip on the back of the neck, and knocked him down. After looking at him for a moment, he got on his horse again and rode back to town. I went out to see if Tommy was dead, and as he still moved, I finished him, for he was always in mischief. Just then I saw Mr. Muspius coming, so I put Tommy up against the fence with his head through, to hold him up, and returned to the kitchen. Mr. Muspius looked round when he got off and saw Tommy, so he gave him a flick with the double of the stock-whip he was carrying, and Tommy tumbled down. He thought he'd killed him, for he got on his horse again and rode away just the same as Mr. Vaughan. I put poor Tommy up again with his head through the fence, and then Mr. Lawrence came along. 'There's that d— emu,' he said, 'trying to get into the garden;' and he picked up a stick and threw it at him, and down went Tommy. I came out and looked at him and he looked at me. 'My word,' I said, 'Missee Lawrence make a fuss.' 'Hush,' he said, 'you no savee anything'; and he gave me a pound—and he went in and tell Missee some 'bomniable wletch' killed Tommy.

That afternoon I went into Wattleville, and Mr. Muspius gave me a pound not to tell, and Mr. Vaughan gave me another. Then, in the evening, Missee Lawrence came into the kitchen and said: 'Ah Foo, I'm going to Sydney tomorrow to get married. Here's a pound to bury poor Tommy properly.'

Next morning, young Wilson, the new-chum from the next station, came over, and he said, when he saw Tommy: 'Ah Foo, I want an emu-skin to send home to England to say I shot him. You skin me this nicely and I'll give you a pound.'

That welly good emu, that makee me flive pounds.

A HAUNT OF THE JINKARRAS
(A STORY OF CENTRAL AUSTRALIA)

In May, 1889, the dead body of a man was found on one of the tributaries of the Finke River, in the extreme North of South Australia. The body, by all appearances, had been lying there for months and was accidentally discovered by some surveyors making a flying survey with camels. Amongst the few effects was a diary containing the following narrative, which, although in many places almost illegible and much weather-stained, has been since, with some trouble, deciphered and transcribed by the surveyor in charge of the party.

Transcribed from the Dead Man's Diary.

MARCH 10, 1888.—Started out this morning with Jackson, who is the only survivor of a party of three who lost their horses on a dry stage when looking for country; he was found and cared for by the blacks, and finally made his way into the telegraph-line, where I picked him up when out with a repairing-party. Since then I got him a job on the station, and in return he has told me about the ruby-field of which we are now in search; thanks to the late thunder-storms we have as yet met with no obstacles to our progress. I have great faith in him as a bushman, but being a man without any education and naturally taciturn, he is not very lively company, and I find myself thrown on to the resource of a diary for amusement.

March 17.—Seven days since we left Charlotte Waters, and we are now approaching the country familiar to Jackson during his sojourn with the natives two years ago. He is confident that we shall gain the gorge in the M'Donnell Ranges to-morrow, early.

March 18.—Amongst the ranges, plenty of water, and Jackson has recognised several peaks in the near neighbourhood of the gorge, where he saw the rubies.

March 19.—Camped in Ruby Gorge, as I have named this pass, for we have come straight to the place and found the rubies without any hindrance at all. I have about twenty magnificent stones and hundreds of small ones; one of the stones in particular is almost living fire, and must be of great value. Jackson has no idea of the value of the find, except that it may be worth a few pounds, with which he will be quite satisfied. As there is good feed and water, and we have plenty of rations, will camp here for a day or two and spell the horses before returning.

March 20.—Been inspecting some caves in the ranges. One of them seems to penetrate a great distance—will go tomorrow with Jackson and take candles and examine it.

March 25.—Had a terrible experience the last four days. Why did I not return at once with the rubies? Now I may never get back. Jackson and I started to explore the cave early in the morning. We found nothing extraordinary about it for some time. As usual there were numbers of bats, and here and there were marks of fire on the rocks, as though the natives had camped in it at times. After some search, Jackson discovered a passage which we followed down a steep incline for a long distance. As we got on we encountered a strong draught of air and had to be very careful of our candles. Suddenly the passage opened and we found ourselves in a low chamber in which we could scarcely stand upright. I looked hastily around, and saw a dark figure like a large monkey suddenly spring from a rock and disappear with what sounded like a splash. 'What on earth was that?' I said to Jackson. 'A jinkarra,' he replied, in his slow, stolid way. 'I heard about them from the blacks; they live underground.' 'What are they?' I asked. 'I couldn't make out,' he replied; 'the blacks talked about jinkarras, and made signs that they were underground, so I suppose that was one.'

We went over to the place where I had seen the figure and, as the air was now comparatively still and fresh, our candles burnt well and we could see plainly. The splash was no illusion, for an underground stream of some size ran through the chamber, and, on looking closer, in the sand on the floor of the cavern we could see tracks like those of human feet.

We sat down and had something to eat. The water was beautifully fresh and icily cold, and I tried to extract from Jackson all he knew about the jinkarras. It was very little beyond what he had already told me. The natives spoke of them as something, animals or men, he could not make out which, living in the ranges under ground. They used to frighten the children by crying out 'jinkarra!' to them at night.

The stream that flowed through the cavern was very sluggish and apparently not deep, as I could see the white sand at a distance under the rays of the candle; it disappeared beneath a rocky arch about two feet above its surface. Strange to say, when near this place I could detect a peculiar smell as of something burning, and this odour appeared to come through the arch. I drew Jackson's attention to it, and proposed wading down the channel of the stream if not too deep, but he suggested going back to camp first and getting more rations, which being very reasonable, I agreed to.

It took us too long returning to camp to think of starting that day, but next morning we got away early and were soon beside the subterranean stream. The water was bitterly cold but not very deep, and we had provided ourselves with stout saplings as poles and had our revolvers and some rations strapped on our shoulders. It was a nasty wade through the chilly water, our heads nearly touching the slimy top of the arch, our candles throwing a faint, flickering gleam on the surface of the stream. Fortunately the bottom was splendid—hard, smooth sand—and, after wading for about twenty minutes, we suddenly emerged into another cavern, but its extent we could not discern at first, for our attention was taken up with other matters.

The air was laden with pungent smoke, the place illuminated with a score of smouldering fires, and tenanted by a crowd of the most hideous beings

I ever saw. They espied us in an instant, and flew wildly about, jabbering frantically, until we were nearly deafened. Recovering ourselves, we waded out of the water, and tried to approach some of these creatures; but they hid away in the dark corners, and we could not lay hands on any of them. As well as we could make out in the murky light, they were human beings, but savages of the most degraded type, far below that of the common Australian blackfellow. They had long arms, shaggy heads of hair, small twinkling eyes, and were very low of stature. They kept up a confused jabber, half whistling, half chattering, and were utterly without clothes, paint, or any ornaments. I approached one of their fires, and found it to consist of a kind of peat or turf; some small bones of vermin were lying around, and a rude club or two. While gazing at these things I suddenly heard a piercing shriek, and, looking up, found that Jackson, by a sudden spring, had succeeded in capturing one of these creatures, who was struggling and uttering terrible yells. I went to his assistance, and together we succeeded in holding him still while we examined him by the light of our candles. The others, meanwhile, ceased their clamour and watched us curiously.

Never had I seen so repulsive a wretch as our prisoner. Apparently he was a young man about two or three and twenty, hardly five feet high at the outside, lean, with thin legs and long arms. He was trembling all over, and the perspiration dripped from him. He had scarcely any forehead, and a shaggy mass of hair crowned his head, and grew a long way down his spine. His eyes were small, red and bloodshot; I have often experienced the strong odour emitted by aborigines when heated or excited, but never did I meet with anything so offensive as the rank smell emanating from this being. Suddenly Jackson exclaimed: 'Look! look! he's got a tail!' I looked and nearly relaxed my grasp of the brute in surprise. There was no doubt about it, this strange being had about three inches of a monkey-like tail.

'Let's catch another,' I said to Jackson after the first emotion of surprise had passed. We looked around after sticking our candles upright in the sand. 'There's one in the corner,' muttered Jackson to me, and as soon as I saw the one he meant we released our prisoner and made a simultaneous rush at the cowering form. We were successful, and when we dragged our captive to the light we found it to be a woman. Our curiosity was soon satisfied—the tail was the badge of the whole tribe, and we let our second captive go.

My first impulse was to go and rinse my hands in the stream, the contact had been so repulsive to me. It was the same with Jackson. I pondered what I should do. I had a great desire to take one of these singular beings back with me, and I thought with pride of the reputation I should gain as their discoverer. Then I reflected that I could always find them again, and it would be better to come back with a larger party after safely disposing of the rubies and securing the ground.

'There's no way out of this place,' I said to Jackson.

'Think not?' he replied.

'No,' I said, 'or these things would have cleared out; they must know every nook and cranny.'

'Umph!' he said, as though satisfied; 'shall we go back now?'

I was on the point of saying 'yes,' and had I done so all would have been well, but, unfortunately, some motive of infernal curiosity prompted me to say—'No! let us have a look round first.' Lighting another candle each, so that we had plenty of light, we wandered round the cave, which was of considerable extent, the unclean inhabitants flitting before us with beast-like cries. Presently we had made a half-circuit of the cave and were approaching the stream, for we could hear a rushing sound as though it plunged over a fall. This noise grew louder, and now I noticed that all the natives had disappeared and it struck me that they had retreated through the passage we had penetrated, which was now unguarded. Suddenly Jackson, who was ahead, exclaimed that there was a large opening. As he spoke he turned to enter it; I called out to him to be careful, but my voice was lost in a cry of alarm as he slipped, stumbled, and with a shriek of horror disappeared from my view. So sudden was the shock, and so awful my surroundings, that I sank down utterly unnerved, comprehending but one thing: that I was alone in this gruesome cavern inhabited by strange, unnatural creations.

After a while I braced myself up, and began to look about. Holding my candle aloft I crawled on my stomach to the spot whence my companion had disappeared. My hand touched a slippery decline; peering cautiously ahead I saw that the rocks sloped abruptly downwards, and were covered with slime, as though under water at times. One step on the treacherous surface and a man's doom was sealed—headlong into the unknown abyss he was bound to go, and this had been the fate of the unhappy Jackson. As I lay trembling on the edge of this fatal chasm, listening for the faintest sound from below, it struck me that the noise of the rushing water was both louder and nearer. I lay and listened. There was no doubt about it— the waters were rising. With a thrill of deadly horror it flashed across me that if the stream rose it would prevent my return, as I could not thread the subterranean passage under water. Rising hastily I hurried back to the upper end of the cavern, following the edge of the water. A glance assured me I was a prisoner—the flood was up to the top of the arch, and the stream much broader than when we entered. The rations and candles we had left carelessly on the sand had disappeared, covered by the rising water. I was alone, with nothing but about a candle and a half between me and darkness and death.

I blew out the candle, threw myself on the sand and tried to think calmly. I brought all my courage to bear on the prospect before me, so as not to let it daunt me. First, the natives had evidently retreated before the water rose too high, their fires were all out, and a dead silence reigned. I had the cavern to myself, which was better than their horrid company. Next, the rising was periodical, and evidently caused the sliminess of the rock, which had robbed me of my only companion. I remembered instances in the interior where lagoons rose and fell at certain times without any visible cause. Then came the thought—for how long would the overflow continue? I had fresh air and plenty of water, and so I could live for days; probably the flood only lasted twelve or twenty-four hours. But a deadly fear seized on me. Could I maintain my reason in this worse than

Egyptian darkness—a darkness so thick, definite and palpable as to be indescribable, truly a darkness that could be felt? I had heard of men who could not endure twenty-four hours in a dark cell, but had clamoured to be taken out. Supposing my reason deserted me, and during some delirious interlude the stream rose and fell again!

These thoughts were too agonising. I rose and paced a step or two on the sand. I made a resolution during that short walk. I had matches—fortunately, with a bushman's instinct, I had put a box in my pouch when we started to investigate the cavern. I had a candle and a half, and, thank Heaven! my watch. I would calculate four hours as nearly as possible, and every four hours I would strike a match and enjoy the luxury of a little light. I pursued this plan, and by doing so left that devilish pit with my reason. It was sixty hours before the stream fell, and what I suffered during that time no tongue can tell, no brain imagine.

That awful darkness was at times peopled by forms which, for hideousness, no nightmare could surpass. Invisible, but still present, they surrounded and sought to drive me down the chasm wherein my companion had fallen. The loathsome inhabitants of that cavern came back in fancy and gibbered and whistled around me. I could smell them—feel their sickening touch. If I slept I awoke from, perhaps a pleasant dream to the stern fact that I was alone in darkness in the depth of the earth. When first I found that the water was receding was perhaps the hardest time of all, for my anxiety to leave the chamber tenanted by such phantoms was overpowering. But I resisted. I held to my will until I knew I could safely venture, and then waded slowly and determinedly up the stream; up the sloping passage, through the outer cave, and emerged in the light of day—the blessed, glorious light, with a wild shout of joy.

I must have fainted: when I came to myself I was still at the mouth of the cave, but now it was night, the bright, starlit, lonely, silent night of the Australian desert. I felt no hunger nor fear of the future; one delicious sense of rest and relief thrilled my whole being. I lay there watching the dearly-loved Austral constellations in simple, peaceful ecstasy. And then I slept, slept till the sun aroused me, and I took my way to our deserted camp. A few crows arose and cawed defiantly at me, and the leather straps bore the marks of a dingo's teeth, otherwise the camp was untouched. I lit a fire, cooked a meal, ate, and rested once more. The reaction had set in after the intense strain I had endured, and I felt myself incapable of thinking or purposing anything. This state lasted for four-and-twenty hours—then I awoke to the fact that I had to find the horses, and make my way home alone—for, alas, as I bitterly thought, I was now, through my curiosity, alone, and, worst of all had been the cause of my companion's death. Had I come away when he proposed, he would be alive, and I should have escaped the terrible experience I have endured.

I have written this down while it is fresh in my memory; to-morrow I start to look for the horses. If I reach the telegraph-line safely I will come back and follow up the discovery of this unknown race, the connecting and long-sought-for link; if not, somebody else may find this and follow up the clue. I have plotted out the course from Charlotte Waters here by dead-reckoning.

March 26th.—No sign of the horses. They have evidently made back. I will make up a light pack and follow them. If I do not overtake them I may be able to get on to the line on foot. The stages between the water-holes on our way out were not very long, and I ought to manage it safely.

End of the Diary

NOTE.—The surveyor, who is well-known in South Australia, adds the following postscript:—

> The unfortunate man was identified as an operator on the overland line. He had been in the service a long time, and was very much liked. The facts about picking up Jackson when out with a repairing party have also been verified. The dead man had obtained six months' leave of absence, and it was supposed he had gone down to Adelaide. The tradition of jinkarras us common among the natives of the McDonnell Range. I have often heard it. No rubies or anything of value were found on the body.

TRANTER'S SHOT

'I SHOT him like a dog!' said Tranter, as he got off his horse and proceeded to unsaddle.

'Whom did you shoot?' asked the new superintendent, who was standing by.

'Never mind,' returned Tranter. 'I'm not going to give myself away, but I shot him like a dog.'

There was bad blood between Tranter and the new super., and, as Tranter was about to leave, he was far from respectful in his manner.

The new super. was a young man from the South, and Tranter was an old Gulf hand. The new super. was a black-protector and temperance-advocate, and objected to swearing. Tranter, to sustain his character as an old Gulf hand, swore the most blood-curdling oaths in his presence, and told the most awful lies he could invent about black atrocities. Consequently, they fell out, and Tranter was leaving the station.

'Now, look here,' said the super., 'I'll get to the bottom of this—I'll just follow your tracks and find out what you have been up to.'

'You'll find him safe enough,' said Tranter, '*he* won't get away.'

The wrathful superintendent had his horse brought up, and started back on Tranter's track, taking another man with him. The trail was not hard to follow, as Tranter had been after horses and they had come home along a cattle-track.

The two had gone about five miles when a loud, wailing cry suddenly startled them. They were in scrubby country at the foot of a low conglomerate rise, with many boulders strewn about.

Following the direction of the cry, they came to an old gin seated on the ground cutting herself, or endeavouring to do so, with a piece of broken glass, and occasionally uttering the wail that had first attracted their notice. Green, the super., knew that this was a sign of mourning, and guessed that he was on the right track.

'There's been murder here,' he said, dismounting and approaching the gin. She took no notice of them, but kept on moaning and scraping at her breast.

'Let's look about,' said the man, 'they always go on like this, and we can't stop her.'

They searched a while without result, the gin still maintaining her lamentation. Then Green, having made up his mind that a vile outrage had been committed, remounted, and they cantered back to the station.

'I will get F——,' he said, naming the native-police inspector, 'to bring a trooper and search.'

The 'barracks' were only some three miles from the station, and F—— was soon up there with his smartest tracker.

Meantime, Green had been trying to extract from Tranter what he had done with the body of his victim.

'I shot him like a dog, and I buried him like a dog,' was all he could obtain in answer. 'Go and find him, *he* won't run away.'

Green was infuriated, but he knew he could do nothing until evidence of the murder was established.

With one delay and another it was late in the afternoon ere Green, F——, and the black trooper arrived at the scene of the tragedy. The old gin was still sitting there raising her requiem song, but the black boy could obtain no information from her.

'Some fellow bin go bung,' was all he was assured of.

They searched without avail until dusk, and then had to depart unsatisfied, the most astonishing thing being that they could find no tracks of blacks other than those of the gin. Green took counsel with F——, but the latter could say nothing, except that the fact of the presence of the gin sounding the death-wail and Tranter's boasting were not sufficient evidence to obtain a warrant on. For himself he thought, from what he had seen, that Tranter had shot a blackfellow there, but his mere belief would go for nothing. However, he slept at the station and promised to renew the search as early as possible.

Green passed a sleepless night. Here was a chance right into his hands of vindicating his opinions as to the murderous treatment of the natives, and he seemed most unaccountably baffled. He vowed that he would leave no stone unturned on the morrow, and at daylight fell asleep and slept so long that it was late when they got away.

Arrived at the fatal spot they at once set to work and began to examine the ground. The old gin had gone back to camp, and they were undisturbed by her outcries. Green had brought two men with him, so they were a strong party.

Suddenly the black trooper stopped and stamped his foot. 'What for me —— fool?' he exclaimed. 'Me know what that fellow shoot!'

'What?' cried the others, crowding round.

'You know, can't find em track—only old gin's track.'

'Yes.'

'Of course, that one shoot em piccaniny. Gin bin carry it.'

This probable solution, so much more horrible than they had expected, struck them all as the true one, and they hastened to the spot where the old native woman had been squatting. The trooper set to work and rolled away the boulder she had been leaning against, then he threw out some of the smaller stones, and, putting down his hand, drew forth by one leg the ghastly object of their search—the corpse of a fine fat dog, evidently the late property of the lamenting lubra.

Tranter was even with the super., who never got over the chaff, but returned south.

SPIRIT-LED

I.

IT was the hottest day the Gulf[1] had seen for years. Burning, scorching and blistering heat, beating down directly from the vertical sun, in the open; radiating from the iron roof which provided what was mistakenly called shade. In the whole township there was not a corner to be found where a man could escape the suffocating sense of being in the stoke-hole of a steamer.

The surroundings were not of a nature to be grateful to eyes wearied with the monotony of plain and forest. The few stunted trees that had been spared seemed to sadly regret not having shared the fate of their comrades, and the barren ironstone ridge on which the township was built gave back with interest all the sun's heat it had absorbed.

Two men were seated on canvas chairs in the verandah of one of the principal 'hotels,' both lightly attired in shirt and trousers only, busily engaged in mopping the perspiration from their steaming faces, and swearing at the flies.

'Deuced sight hotter lounging about here than travelling,' said Davis, the elder of the two; 'I vote we make a start.'

'I'm agreeable,' replied his companion; 'the horses must be starving in the paddock. But we shall have a job to get Delaine away, he's bent on seeing his cheque through.'

---

[1] Gulf of Carpentaria.

'That won't take long at the rate he's going. He's got every loafer in the town hanging about him.'

'Hullo! what's that?' said the other, as the shrill whistle of a steam-launch was heard. 'Oh! of course, the steamer arrived at the mouth of the river last night; that's the launch coming up. Shall we go down and see who is on board?'

The two men got up and joined the stragglers who were wending their way across the bare flat to the bank of the river. Some of the passengers were strangers to the place; one of them, a man with white hair and beard, though otherwise young-looking, immediately attracted Davis' attention.

'See that chap, Bennett?' he said.

'Yes, Dick, who is he?'

'Some years ago he was with me on a droving trip; when we started he was a fine fellow with dark hair. It's a true bill about a man's hair going white in one night. His did.'

'What from? Fright?'

'Yes. We nearly buried him alive by mistake.'

'The deuce you did!'

'He had a cataleptic fit on watch one night. The other man—we were double-banking the watch at the time—found him as stiff as a poker, and we all thought he was dead, there were no signs of life in him. It was hot weather—as bad as this—and we couldn't keep him, so we dug a grave, and started to bury him at sundown. He came to when we were filling in the grave, yelled blue murder, and frightened the life out of us. His hair that night turned as you see it now, although he vows it was not the fright of being buried alive that did it.'

'What then?'

'Something that happened when he was in the fit, or trance. He has never said more than that he was perfectly conscious all the time, and had a very strange experience.'

'Ever ask him anything?'

'No, he didn't like talking about it. Wonder what he's doing up here?'

By this time the river bank was deserted. Davis and Bennett strolled up after the others, and on arrival at the hotel found the hero of the yarn there before them.

'Hullo, Maxwell,' said Davis, 'what brought you up this way?'

Maxwell started slightly when he saw his quondam sexton, but he met him frankly enough, although, at first, he disregarded the question that had been asked.

In the course of the conversation that followed, Maxwell stated that he was on his way out to the Nicholson river, but with what object did not transpire.

'Bennett and I were just talking of making a start to-morrow, or the next day. Our cattle are spelling on some country just this side of the river. You had better come with us.'

'I shall be very glad,' replied the other, and the thing was settled.

Bennett had been looking curiously at this man who had had so narrow an escape, but beyond the strange whiteness of his hair (which contrasted oddly with the swarthy hue of his sunburnt face) and a nervous look in his eyes, he showed no trace of his singular experience. On the contrary, he promised, upon nearer acquaintance, to be a pleasant travelling companion.

The next morning broke hot and sullen as before. Davis had risen early to send a man out to the paddock after the horses, and was in the bar, talking to the landlord.

'You'll have to knock off his grog or there'll be trouble,' he said. 'He was up all last night wandering about with his belt and revolver on, muttering to himself, and when a fellow does that he's "got 'em" pretty bad.'

'I'll do what I can, but if he doesn't get drink here he will somewhere else,' replied the publican, reluctantly.

'Then I'll see the magistrate and ask him to prohibit his being served. It's the only way to get him straight.'

At this moment the subject of their remarks entered the bar—a young fellow about five or six and twenty—who evidently had not been in bed all night. The whites of his eyes were not blood-shot, but blood-red throughout, and the pupils so dilated that they imparted a look of unnatural horror to his face.

'Hullo, Davis!' he shouted; 'glad to see a white man at last. That old nigger with the white hair has been after me all night—the old buck who was potted in the head. He comes along every night now with his flour-bag cobra[2] all over blood. Can't get a wink of sleep for him. Have a drink?'

His speech was quite distinct, he was past the stage when strong waters thicken the voice; his walk was steady, and but for the wild eyes, he might have passed for a man who was simply tired out with a night's riding or watching.

The landlord glanced enquiringly at Davis, as if to put on him the responsibility of serving the liquor.

'Too early, Delaine, and too hot already; besides, I'm going to start to-day and mustn't get tight before breakfast,' said the latter soothingly.

'Oh, be hanged! Here, give us something,' and the young fellow turned towards the bar, and as he did so caught sight of Maxwell, who had just come to the door and was looking in.

The effect on his excited brain of seeing the dark face and snow-white hair was awful to witness. His eyes, blazing before, seemed now simply orbs of fire. Davis and the landlord turned to see what the madman was looking at, and that moment was nearly fatal to the newcomer. Muttering: 'By ——, he's taken to following me by daylight as well, has he? But I'll soon stop him!' he drew his revolver and, only that Davis turned his head again and was just in time to knock his hand up, Maxwell would have been past praying for. The landlord ran round the bar, and with some trouble the three men got the pistol from the maniac, who raved, bit, and fought like a wild beast. The doctor, who slept in the house, was called,

---

[2] White head.

34

and injected some morphia into the patient's arm, which soon sent him into a stupor.

'By jove, Davis, you saved my life,' said Maxwell; 'that blessed lunatic would have shot me sure enough only for you. Whom did he take me for?'

'He's got the horrors, his name is Delaine, and he's from a station on the tableland. They had some trouble with the blacks up there lately, and, I suppose, it was the first dispersing-match[3] he had ever seen. There was one white-haired old man got a bullet through his head, and he says he felt as though his own father had been shot when he saw it done. He's a clergyman's son, so, of course, he drinks like a fish, and is superstitious as well.'

'I trust they'll lock him up until I get out of the town; but I'll remember your share of this. Wait until we get away and I will tell you what brought me up here, but don't ask me any questions now. Is your friend Bennett to be trusted?'

'In what way? Wine, women, or gold? I don't know about the first two, but the last I can answer for.'

'It's a secret. Possibly connected with the last.'

'I hope so, I want some badly enough. I think I know where to put you on to a couple of good horses, and then we'll make a start.'

II.

The stove-like township is three days' journey away; four men, Davis, Bennett, Maxwell, and a blackfellow, are camped for the night by the side of a small lagoon covered with the broad leaves of the purple water-lily. In the distance the cheery sound of horse-bells can be heard, and round the fire the travellers are grouped listening to Maxwell, who is telling the tale he has never yet told:

---

[3] Nigger raid.

'When I fell down on watch that night and became to all appearance a corpse, I never, for one instant, lost either consciousness or memory. My soul, spirit, or whatever you like to call it, parted company with my body, but I retained all former powers of observation. I gazed at myself lying there motionless, waited until my fellow-watcher came around and awakened the sleeping camp with the tidings of my death; then, without any impulse of my own, I left the spot and found myself in a shadowy realm where all was vague and confused. Strange, indistinct shapes flitted constantly before me, I heard voices and sounds like sobbing and weeping.

'Now, before I go any further, let me tell you that I have never been subject to these fits. I never studied any occult arts, nor troubled myself about what I called 'such rubbish.' Why this experience should have befallen me I cannot say. I found I was travelling along swiftly, carried on by some unknown motive power, or, rather, drifting aimlessly with a current of misty forms in which all seemed confusion. Suddenly, to my surprise, I found myself on the earth once more, in a place quite unknown to me.

'I was in Australia—that much I recognised at a glance—but whereabouts?

'I was standing on the bank of a river—a northern river, evidently, for I could see the foliage of the drooping ti-trees and Leichhardt trees further down its course. The surrounding country was open, but barren; immediately in front of me was a rugged range through which the river found its way by means of an apparently impenetrable gorge. The black rocks rose abruptly on either side of a deep pool of water, and all progress, except by swimming, was barred. On both sides the ranges were precipitous, cleft by deep ravines; all the growth to be seen was spinifex, save a few stunted bloodwood trees.

'What struck me most forcibly was, that in the centre of the water-hole, at the entrance of the gorge, there arose two rocks, like pillars, some twelve or fifteen feet above the surface of the water.

'Below the gorge the river-bed was sandy, and the usual timber grew on the banks. At first I thought I was alone, but, looking round, I found that a man was standing a short distance away from me. Apparently he was a European, but so tanned and burnt by the sun as to be almost copper-coloured. He was partially clothed in skins, and held some hunting-weapons in his hand. He was gazing absently into the gorge when I first noticed him, but presently turned, and, without evincing any surprise or curiosity, beckoned to me. Immediately, in obedience to some strange impulse, I found myself threading the gloomy gorge with him, although, apparently, we exercised no motion. It was more as though we stood still and the rocks glided past us and the water beneath us. We soon reached a small open space or pocket; here there was a rude hut, and we halted.

'My strange companion looked around and, without speaking, drew my attention to a huge boulder close to the hut, on which letters and figures were carved. I made out the principal inscription:—

Hendrik Heermans, her vangecommen, 1670.

There were also an anchor, a ship and a heart, all neatly cut. I turned from these records to the man. He beckoned me again; I followed him across the small open space and up a ravine. The man pointed to a reef cropping out and crossing the gully. I looked at it and saw that the cap had been broken and that gold was showing freely in the stone. The man waved his hand up the gully as though intimating that there were more reefs there.

'Suddenly, sweeping up the gorge came a gust of ice-cold wind, and with it a dash of mist or spray. Looming out of this I saw for a moment a young girl's face looking at me. Her lips moved. 'Go back. Go back!' she seemed to whisper.

'When I heard this I felt an irresistible longing to return to my discarded body, and, in an instant, gorge, mountains and all my surroundings disappeared, and I found myself in the twilight space battling despairingly on, for I felt that I had lost my way and should never find it again.

'How was I to reach my forsaken body through such a vague, misty and indeterminate land? Impalpable forms threw themselves in my path.

Strange cries and wailings led me astray, and all the while there was a smell as of death in my nostrils, and I knew that I must return or die.

'Oh, the unutterable anguish of that time! Ages seemed to pass during which I was fighting with shadows, until at last, I saw a sinking sun, an open grave, and men whose faces I knew, commencing to shovel earth on a senseless body.

'Mine!

'I had felt no pain when my soul left, but the re-entrance of it into its tenement was such infinite agony, that it forced from me terrible cries that caused my rescue from suffocation.'

Maxwell paused, and the other two were silent.

'You will wonder,' he resumed, 'what all this has to do with my present journey. I will tell you. You remember Milford, a surveyor up here—at one time he was running the boundary-line between Queensland and South Australia for the Queensland Government? A year ago I met him, and we were talking about the country up this way. In running the line he had to follow the Nicholson a good way, until finally he was completely blocked. He described to me the place where he had to turn back. It was the water-hole in the gorge with the two rock-like pillars rising out of the water.'

Again there was silence for a while. Then Davis said musingly—

'It's impossible to pronounce any opinion at present; the coincidence of Milford's report is certainly startling. But why should this sign have been vouchsafed to you? Apparently this being you saw was the ghost of some old Dutch sailor wrecked or marooned here in the days of the early discovery of Australia. Had you any ancestors among those gentry?'

'Not that I am aware of,' returned Maxwell, 'but if we find the place we shall certainly make some interesting discovery, apart from any gold.'

'And the girl's face?' enquired Bennett.

Maxwell did not answer for a minute or two.

'I may as well tell you all,' he said then; 'I was in Melbourne, after I saw Milford, and I met a girl with that same face, in the street. Strange, too, we could not help looking at each other as though we knew we had met before. That meeting decided me on taking the trip up here. Now, that is really all. Are you ready for the adventure?'

'I should think so,' said Davis, 'we have fresh horses at the camp, and nothing to do with ourselves for three months or more. Please God, we'll soon be on Tom Tiddler's ground picking up gold in chunks.'

'One question more,' put in Bennett. 'Have you ever had any return of these trances or cataleptic fits?'

'Never since, not the slightest sign of one.'

III.

There was no doubt about the strange proof or coincidence, whichever it should turn out to be. The three men stood on the bank of the Nicholson gazing at the gorge and the water-hole, from the bosom of which rose the two upright pillars of rock. A fortnight had elapsed since they were camped at the lagoon.

'It's the same place,' muttered Maxwell—and, as the overwhelming horror of his fight through shadowland came back to him, he leant on his horse's shoulder and bowed his head down on the mane.

Bennett made a sign to Davis, and both were silent for a while. Then Davis spoke—

'Well, old man, as we aren't possessed of the supernatural power you had when you were last here, we'll have to get over that range somehow.'

Maxwell lifted his head. 'We must tackle the range, but I expect we shall have a job to get the horses over. How about leaving them here in hobbles and going up on foot?'

'Not to be thought of,' replied Davis; 'why, the niggers' tracks just back there in the bed of the river are as thick as sheep-tracks. The horses would be speared before we got five miles away. I know these beggars.'

'That's true,' said Bennett.

Davis eyed the range curiously for some time. 'There's a spur there that we can work our way up, I think,' he said at last, indicating with his hand the spot he meant. The other two, after a short inspection, agreed with him. It was then nearly noon, so the horses were turned out for a couple of hours' spell, a fire lit and the billy boiled.

'What could have led your Dutch sailor up this way?' said Davis as, the meal over, they were enjoying a pipe.

'That is what has puzzled me. I have read up everything I could get hold of on the subject of Dutch discovery and can find no record of any ship visiting the Gulf about that date,' replied Maxwell.

'There may have been plenty of ships here, of which neither captain nor crew wanted a record kept. Those were the days of the buccaneers,' said Bennett.

'Yes, but with the exception of the ship which had Dampier on board, they did not come out of their way to New Holland,' returned Maxwell.

'The *Bachelor's Delight* and the *Cygnet* were on the west coast, as you say; why not others which had not the luck to be associated with Dampier?'

'True; but the Dutch were not noted as buccaneers. However, plenty of ships may have been lost in the Gulf of which all record has disappeared. The question is, what brought the man up into this region?' said Davis.

'I firmly believe we shall get the clue to that secret when we find the ravine. It seems incredible that a shipwrecked or marooned man should have left the seacoast, whereon was his only hope of salvation, and have made south into an unknown land, through such a range as this.'

'Well, boys, we'll make a start for it,' said Davis, jumping up; and the party were soon in their saddles.

The range proved stiff climbing, and they were so often baulked, and forced to retrace their steps, that it was sundown ere they reached the top.

*   *   *

It was a desolate outlook for a camp. A rough tableland of spinifex—evidently extending too far for them to cross and descend the other side before darkness set in—lay before them.

'Nothing for it but to go on and tie the horses up all night,' said Bennett. Fortune, however, favoured them; in about a mile they came to a small patch of grass, sufficient for the horses, and as their water-bags were full, they gladly turned out.

*   *   *

'Well, Maxwell,' said Davis, as they were discussing breakfast, 'hear anything from your old Dutch navigator last night?'

'No, only I had some confused sort of dream about this place; I thought I heard that voice once more telling me to 'go back.' But that, of course, is only natural.'

'I think we are close to the spot,' remarked Bennett. 'When I was after the horses this morning I could see down into the river, and there appeared to be a pocket there.'

Bennett proved right. In half-an-hour's time they were scrambling down the range, and soon stood in an open space which Maxwell at once identified.

Naturally everyone was somewhat excited. Although at first inclined to put the story down to hallucination, the subsequent events had certainly shaken this belief in the minds of the two friends. Maxwell silently pointed to the boulder; there was something carved on it, but it was worn and indistinct. Two centuries of weather had almost obliterated whatever marks had been there.

'They were fresh and clear when I saw them,' said Maxwell, in an awed voice.

By diligent scrutiny they made out the inscription that he had formerly repeated, but had they not known it the task would have been most difficult. The words had not been very deeply marked, and as the face of the boulder fronted north-west, the full force of two hundred years' monsoons had been experienced by the inscription.

'This is a wonderful thing,' said Davis. 'There can be no doubt as to its age.'

'Let's go up the ravine and look for the reef and then get back as soon as possible. I don't like this place. I wish I had not come,' returned Maxwell.

They left the pack-horses feeding about and rode up the gully, taking with them the pick and shovel they had brought. 'It was here, I think,' said Maxwell, looking round, 'but the place seems altered.'

'Very likely the creek would change its course slightly in a couple of hundred years, but not much. That looks like an outcrop there.'

'This is the place,' replied Maxwell, eagerly, 'I know it now, but it is a little different.'

The three dismounted, and Davis, taking the pick, struck the cap of the reef, breaking off some lumps of stone. As he did so, a wild 'Holloa!' rang up the gully. All started and looked at each other with faces suddenly white and hearts quickly beating. There was something grisly in such a cry arising out of the surrounding solitude.

'Blacks?' said Bennett, doubtfully. Davis shook his head. Once more the loud shout was raised, apparently coming from the direction of the inscribed rock.

'Let's go and see what it is, anyhow,' said Davis—and they mounted and rode down the gully again, Bennett, who had picked up a piece of the quartz, putting it into his saddle-pouch as they went along.

Maxwell had not spoken since the cry had been heard, his face was pale, and occasionally he muttered to himself, 'Go back, go back!' The pack-horses were industriously cropping what scanty grass there was; all seemed peaceful and quiet.

'I believe it was a bird, after all; there's a kind of toucan makes a devil of a row—have a look round,' said Davis to Bennett, and they both rode up and down the bank of the river, leaving Maxwell standing near the rock where he had dismounted. Nothing could be seen, and the two returned and proposed going up the gully again.

'You fellows go and come back quickly, I want to get out of this—I'm upset,' said Maxwell in a constrained voice, speaking for the first time.

Davis glanced at his friend. 'Right you are, old man, no wonder you don't feel well; we'll just make sure of the reef and come back. If you want us, fire your pistol; we sha'n't be far off.'

The two rode back to their interrupted work, and hastily commenced their examination of the stone. There was no doubt about the richness of the find, and the reef could be traced a good distance without much trouble. They had collected a small heap of specimens to take back, when suddenly the loud 'Holloa!' came pealing once more up the gully, followed instantly by a fainter cry and two revolver-shots.

Hastily mounting, the two galloped back.

The pack-horses, as if startled, were walking along their tracks towards home, followed by Maxwell's horse with the bridle trailing. Its rider was stretched on the ground; nothing else was visible.

Jumping from their horses they approached the prostrate man. Both started and stared at each other with terror-stricken eyes. Before them lay a skeleton clad in Maxwell's clothes.

'Are we mad?' cried Davis, aghast with horror.

The fierce sun was above them, the bare mountains around, they could hear the horses clattering up the range as if anxious to leave the accursed place, and before them lay a skeleton with the shrunken skin still adhering to it in places—a corpse that had been rotting for years, that had relapsed into the state in which it would have been had the former trance been death. Blind terror seized them both, and they mounted to follow the horses, when an awful voice came from the fleshless lips: 'Stay with me, stop! I may come back; I may—'

Bennett could bear no more, he stuck spurs in his horse and galloped off. Davis would have followed, but he was transfixed with terror at what he saw. The awful object was moving, the outcast spirit was striving desperately to reanimate the body, that had suddenly fallen into decay. The watcher was chained to the spot. Once it seemed that the horrible thing was really going to rise, but the struggle was unavailing; with a loud moan of keenest agony and despair that thrilled the listener's brain with terror, it fell back silent and motionless. Davis remembered nothing more till he found himself urging his horse up the range.

In an asylum for the insane in a Queensland town there is a patient named Bennett, who is always talking about the wonderful reef he knows of up North. He has a specimen of very rich quartz, which he never parts with day or night.

He is often visited by a friend named Davis, who nursed him through a severe attack of fever out on the Nicholson. The doctors think he may yet recover.

THE MYSTERY OF BAINES' DOG

Prologue

THE trouble was first caused by the Malingerites, and, needless to say, it was a case of *cherchez la femme*. One of the youthful members of that tribe had forcibly abducted a maiden of the clan of Layovah, and red war ensued. The worst of it was that they selected as convincing ground a spot close to a much-frequented cattle-camp, on the boundary of two large runs where the herds met. This greatly extended the circle of commotion. The noise and tumult of battle, 'the thunder of the captains and their shouting,' coupled with the shrill yells of the gins, were enough to unsettle the temper of any well-regulated beast, and at the end of the engagement the casualties were—one blackfellow seriously injured by falling over a stump during the heat of combat, two slightly scratched, and one gin very hoarse through screeching. The cattle scattered to the four winds. Most of the Seldon Downs beasts fled on to Inverlochy, and most of the Inverlochy ones to Seldon Downs—all vowing in their bovine hearts never again to set foot on that camp.

So two stations, whereon the owners had dwelt for years in peace and amity, fell out on account of an obscure aboriginal quarrel. Jack Bell, of Seldon Downs, said it was the fault of Tom Devine, who should have kept *his* niggers in better order; and Devine said that Bell knew as much about managing blacks as he did about squaring the circle. The cattle were soon mustered and put right; but the remarks were repeated and remembered.

The two erstwhile friends were in this embittered state when Baines, the hawker, was murdered at the old boundary hut. Then the smouldering feud broke out. Devine maintained that it was evident the man had been killed by the natives on Bell's station; and Bell held as his salvation that the unfortunate fellow met his death at the hands of whites, probably some men lately discharged from Devine's. So the matter stood when our story opens, and the ends of justice were finally defeated because the Malingerites quarrelled with the Layovahs. It is as well to trace things back to their first cause.

I.

Dick Baines, the hawker, had been murdered; of that there was no manner of doubt. He had camped at the boundary-hut, an old, deserted sheep-station, and a traveller passing the next day found him lying alongside his dray with his head cut open. His own axe, with a blood-stained blade, lay beside the body. Evidently he could not have done it himself. On that point everyone agreed.

His horses were safe and his goods apparently untouched, and herein lay the mystery of the crime. He had only just started on his round with a full load, and what little money he had taken was found on his body. There seemed no motive for a white man to commit the deed, and if any of the blacks had done it, why had they not sacked the dray? It was an enigma worthy of a first-class detective-story. Meantime, during its elucidation, there was nothing to do but hold an inquest over what was once Baines, bury it, and let the law do the rest.

The deceased had been some time in the district, and was noted for his reserved manner. He always travelled and camped alone, and seldom drank. He was not extremely popular, and most people suspected that he had 'a past.' One singular feature of the tragedy was that his dog, a smart little fox-terrier, had disappeared. The matter had almost run the orthodox nine days, when interest in it was suddenly revived by the arrest of a man in the small township of Boolah, a short distance from the scene of the murder, who was formally charged with the crime. He had Baines' dog with him.

McFarlane, the man accused, was well known in the district and bore an excellent character. He had been working at Devine's on a fencing contract and had been paid off and left the morning before the hawker was killed. Had started for Seldon Downs, the road to which led past the boundary-hut. Thence he had gone round by two other stations to Boolah. He stated that he found the dog astray in the township, recognised it as the missing animal, called it by name, and the dog followed him. He was about to inform the police when he was arrested by the sergeant.

Scarcely had the surprise occasioned by this been well digested, before a more astonishing one turned up. Baines' dog was also found in a blacks' camp on Seldon Downs.

One of the men riding by the camp noticed a gin scuttling away with something in her arms that yelped and struggled. Rounding her up, he found she was vainly trying to conceal Baines' well-known and apparently ubiquitous dog. Further search revealed nothing more, and the gin made the astounding assertion that the dog had been given to her by a white woman. Beyond that no intelligible information could be elicited from her. The blacks were well watched and the dog taken down to Boolah, where McFarlane was to appear before the magistrates' court.

It now transpired that there were two dogs marked exactly the same, identical in size and appearance, and both answering to the name of 'Rattler.' But the question was, which of the pair was Baines' dog? Never since the judgment of Solomon had law-court a more knotty problem. The animals on being introduced promptly fell on each other tooth and claw and were with difficulty separated. Bell and Devine, both J's. P., were sitting on the bench with the police-magistrate. They differed in opinion. Bell declared that the dog found with McFarlane was the dead hawker's; Devine was equally confident that the dog found on Seldon Downs was the one wanted. After much heated discussion Bell left the bench and desired to give evidence.

He stated that the last time he saw Baines, the hawker showed him a trick he had been teaching his dog. It was an old and well-known performance.

The dog sat up on his hind legs with a piece of meat or biscuit balanced on the tip of his nose; at the words 'ready, present, *fire!*' he tossed it up, caught and swallowed it, and dropped on all fours again. Bell selected the dog he thought was the hawker's, and put him through the performance amidst the hushed attention of a crowded court-room. It was a complete success and he looked up with an air of triumph.

'Yes. That's the dog found on Seldon Downs,' said Devine from the bench.

'Nothing of the sort,' returned Bell hotly, forgetting his position as witness. 'It's the dog found with McFarlane.'

Devine was indignantly replying, when the P.M. interfered and asked the sergeant which dog it was. The sergeant looked at the dogs, then at the two policemen, and they looked blankly back at the sergeant. Then the truth burst upon everybody with such suddenness that a roar of laughter convulsed the court.

The two dogs had got so irretrievably mixed up in the fight that now no one could tell one from the other.

When order was restored (Bell and Devine had nearly come to blows) the P.M. decided to remand the case for a week. Bail was allowed McFarlane, which Devine readily found. One of the dogs, the one which could perform the trick, was ordered to have a collar put on for distinction, and both were given in charge of the lock-up keeper. The enquiry had simply complicated matters. Baines' dog was identified, but nobody could say for certain at which place it had been found. Bell and Devine were, of course, equally positive, but that was mere party feeling. Most people believed in McFarlane's innocence, but Bell vowed that he would bring the murder home to him.

'Can you recall anything suspicious the night you passed Baines?' said Devine to McFarlane, as they went out after signing the bail bonds.

'No, sir. He had hobbled his horses out and was lighting a fire. I got off, lit my pipe, and stopped yarning for about twenty minutes. Then I went on to Seldon Downs.'

'And from there?'

'I came to Boolah by Thirglemere and Bingledoon. I had been here about two hours when I recognised the dog, and directly after I had coaxed him to follow me I was arrested.'

'From the boundary-hut, going round by Seldon Downs, Thirglemere, and Bingledoon, you made it about eighty miles to here and took your time?'

'I stopped two days at Thirglemere and two at Bingledoon. I was a week coming here altogether.'

'But anyone could ride from the boundary-hut straight in to here in about thirty-five miles.'

'Yes, by the old track, but you have fenced that across now.'

'The wires could be easily strapped down, or cut, for that matter. Let's see, I don't suppose it's been used for years, and there has been no rain since Baines was killed. I'm going to run the old track.'

'Will they let me go with you?'

'I'll fix that,' said Devine—and the next morning the two departed for the old track to the boundary-hut.

During their absence, however, Bell was not idle. He returned to the station, and, after much ado, he had the old gin, from whom the dog had been taken, brought into Boolah. As they arrived Devine and McFarlane rode in, returning from their trip to the old hut.

On being shown the two dogs, the gin immediately claimed the one without the collar as being her property. This was satisfactory, to Bell, at any rate, but at this moment Devine came upon the scene. Disdaining to do more than civilly sneer at the test just gone through, he drew the sergeant on one side and held a short conference with him. The sergeant disappeared with the two dogs; the others waited, Bell scornfully impatient. Presently the two dogs reappeared. On being told to pick out her dog, the gin at once again selected the collarless one.

'That's the other one this time, is it not, Sergeant?' said Devine.

'Yes, sir, I shifted the collar just now.'

'It's not fair!' broke in Bell. 'The poor devil's frightened out of her wits; she picked right the first time, but you've bothered her;' and he marched out of the yard in deep disgust.

When Devine and McFarlane left the township they did not trouble to look for tracks until they were well clear of all the stray animals. When about ten miles away the old bridle-path was quite plain. Both men rode on in silence, scanning the ground carefully; at times, with a low whistle, one would call the other's attention to something he saw. Just as they got within sight of the fence, they pulled up.

'It's plain enough, McFarlane,' said Devine; 'a horse has been ridden along here about the time of the murder.'

McFarlane nodded. 'We shall make sure at the fence,' he answered, and they rode on. It was a wire fence, and where it crossed the track the wires were taut and evidently untampered with. The two turned and rode along the fence in opposite directions. A shout from McFarlane brought Devine back to him. He had come to a panel that bore marks of rough usage, from the way the upper wires sagged.

'The top wires have been strapped down and then brushed across,' said the fencer, pointing to the withered boughs lying about.

'And the horse did not fancy tackling it,' added Devine; 'look how he has been hanging back.' Inside the fence the ground was much more bare and dusty, and the tracks of a horse's stamping hoofs deeply indented were plainly visible.

'Whew!' said McFarlane, getting through the fence, 'look here!' Devine followed him. On a particularly dry and dusty bit of ground was the plain imprint of a boot. There should have been nothing strange in this to make the men stare so intently at it; it was only what they might have expected to find.

Placing his hand on McFarlane's shoulder to steady himself, Devine put his foot down close to the track without actually touching the ground. The difference in size was at once apparent.

'Either a boy or a woman,' said McFarlane. 'And the gin said a woman gave her the dog,' returned the other.

Carefully getting back so as not to deface the tracks the two men mounted and rode a short distance down the fence to where they knew was a small gate. Making for the old bridle-path again, they followed it on towards the hut, McFarlane drawing Devine's attention to the track of a small dog now plainly visible on that of the horse.

They stayed that night at the old sheep-station, but no further evidence rewarded their careful search, beyond the fact that some blacks had camped in the neighbourhood, apparently about the date of the murder. They returned to Boolah in time for Devine to be present at the dog-test, as already narrated. McFarlane met him as he was coming out.

'It has just struck me to whom that second dog belongs,' he said.

'Whose is it?'

'Mrs. Brown's; you know, at Boomerang Creek.'

'By Jove, you're right,' said Devine. 'It must have been stolen from there.'

Devine was doubtful whether to communicate the discovery of the suspicious track to the police or not. Against his better judgment he did so, thinking it his duty. They went out, accompanied by Bell, who volunteered his services, examined the track, and reported that it had been made some time since the hawker's death, and so had nothing to do with that occurrence. In this they were partly prompted by Bell, and partly by the fact that as they had searched for tracks, without success, at the time of the murder, it would never do for them to go back on themselves. Devine cursed himself for a fool, and that was all he could do. When McFarlane's case came on again he was, of course, discharged. The evidence was altogether too slight, and several people came forward and testified to having seen the dog in Boolah before McFarlane's arrival.

'I'll find out about that other dog,' said Devine to himself.

II.

Nearly forty miles from Boolah, on the way to the seaport, in the opposite direction to the scene of the tragedy, stood a wayside public-house, on the bank of a large creek, crossed by the road. Mrs. Brown's, on Boomerang Creek, was noted east and west for its neatness, cleanliness and good accommodation. People travelling stretched a point to make the place for the night's stay. The coach-passengers who grumbled at the meagre fare of the other accommodation-houses were told to wait till they came to Mrs. Brown's. Brown, for there was a Mr. Brown, was devoted to outdoor work, but Mrs. Brown was the presiding genius of comfort indoors, and, therefore, the place was generally known as 'Mrs. Brown's.'

When the Judge was on circuit, he always carefully fell ill for a day or two at Mrs. Brown's. Men from the hot western plains, who had lived for weary months upon pigweed and 'salt-horse,' rested at Mrs. Brown's with calm contentment. Freshest of vegetables, of butter, of eggs, and best of cooking, what could a man with a salt-junk saturated liver want more?

As cheery as her well-kept table was the appearance of the hostess herself, a plump little woman, who perennially had a smile upon her pretty face, and a kindly greeting for everybody. She was devoted to her quiet, easy-going husband, who warmly reciprocated the feeling. A word from Mrs. Brown would steady the most drunken fellow, and when she was in the bar the language of all hands was painfully discreet.

It was at this calm haven of rest that Tom Devine dismounted one evening in his character of amateur detective. He was, of course, well known, and Mrs. Brown, as she flitted in and out of the room seeing after his comfort, kept up a lively flow of chatter.

'I suppose you miss something, Mr. Devine?' she said as she invited him to table.

'Well, no! Everything seems as comfortable as usual, Mrs. Brown.'

'I've lost my dog since you were here last. You remember little Rattler?'

'Of course. Why, that must be your little terrier the police have in Boolah,' said Devine, with infinite hypocrisy.

52

Mrs. Brown nodded and smiled brightly. 'Yes, I only heard of it the other day. I must send up and claim him.'

'How did you lose him?'

'I am not sure. He was stolen, I believe; but we had so many travellers staying here at the time that I don't know whom to suspect.'

'Any women amongst them?' asked Devine, quickly.

'Yes, one. I don't know who she was; she was going with her husband to some station out west.'

'Would you know her again if you saw her?'

Mrs. Brown was positive that she would, and in her turn asked what made Mr. Devine so curious.

'I will tell you,' he said, after a pause. 'You have heard all about the murder of Baines, the hawker? Well, one of the dogs was found in a blacks' camp, and the gin who had it asserts that it was given her by a white woman.'

Mrs. Brown looked down on the table upon which her hand rested. 'I should be sorry to hear that she was mixed up in it, for she seemed to be a very nice person,' she replied.

'But if the gin has told the truth she must have stolen your dog.'

'That is true,' she remarked.

Devine was up at sunrise next morning, after restless dreams about a strange woman who went about stealing dogs and killing hawkers. He strolled out and commenced yarning with Brown, who, bucket in hand, was standing at the milking-yard waiting for the cows.

'The missus has gone down the paddock for them this morning,' he confided to Devine; 'got up very early—she couldn't sleep at all last night.'

At this moment the first of the lowing herd made its appearance. Mrs. Brown was behind on foot, driving them up and leading her horse. One after the other they blundered over the rails that had been carelessly let down at one end only. Mrs. Brown followed, but the horse she was leading suddenly stopped and refused to step over the rails.

'Confound that horse!' said Brown, 'he wouldn't lift his legs over a pack-thread if he could help it.'

Devine did not answer. His thoughts were engrossed in a sudden flash of memory. The horse that obstinately hung back on being required to step over anything! The tracks at the wire fence!

Brown went into the yard and commenced milking. Mrs. Brown having succeeded in getting her horse over the rails, went on to the stable, Devine walking by her side.

'Mrs. Brown,' he said quietly. '*I* know who killed Baines, the hawker.'

She started, stopped, and looked him for one moment in the eyes, read there that he knew the truth, and turned so deadly white that he was afraid she would faint. She recovered herself, however, and walked steadily on to the stable. Stopping at the door she glanced around to see if anybody was within hearing, then said firmly: 'Had I better tell you everything, or go and give myself up to the police?'

'Perhaps you had better tell me,' he replied, after a pause.

'Very well. I will, presently.'

Mrs. Brown went about her work that morning apparently unmoved by any unusual emotion. It was not until nearly noon that she found time and opportunity to see Devine.

Her story, which, for the most part is unfortunately a common one, need not be given in full. She was an orphan brought up on a farm by some distant and not overkind relatives. When only an ignorant girl of eighteen, Baines, who then travelled that district, persuaded her to elope with him under a promise of marriage that he never kept. For two years she lived with him as his wife, until, tired of ill-usage and broken vows, she ran away and took service as a barmaid in a country town, where her husband met and married her.

Fate, unfortunately, brought them to settle close to the district where Baines was now plying his trade. The township of Boolah, however, was his limit, and he had never been to their house until about a week before his death. Then, on recognising his former victim, he revengefully threatened to expose her past life to her husband.

'He was one of those evil-minded men,' she went on, 'who must have something to torture. It was only out of sheer love of cruelty that he threatened me, because he saw I was happy with Brown. He vowed that when he came back from his trip he would do it, and showed me some old letters and photographs of mine which would prove his words. You can fancy my feelings when he left me with this hanging over my head. My home to be broken up, and my husband turned against me! At times I was tempted to confess it all to my husband, but then I should have to admit that I only did it under fear of exposure. I made up my mind that if I could succeed in getting the letters and things from Baines, I would dare him to do his worst, and some days after he left, I started under the pretence of paying a visit to a friend in Boolah, with a mad idea of somehow stealing the letters.

'I overtook him at the old hut, and intended to wait in the scrub until he was asleep; but my little dog, which had followed me, betrayed me when he caught sight of the other one. They were twin puppies, and were called 'Rattler the First' and 'Rattler the Second,' and when I ran away from that wretch I took one with me. I had nothing for it but to come forward when he recognised the dog.

'You may guess what brutal taunts he used towards me, and when, in despair of getting what I wanted, I was going away, he tried to stop me by force. His axe was leaning against the wheel, and I picked it up and dared him to touch me. He laughed, and the next moment I struck him down. I scarcely knew I had done it until I saw him lying there.' She stopped, and, after a pause went on:

'My first thought, of course, was to get away; then I remembered my letters. The deed was done, I might as well get what I came for. I soon found the letters and things, and left the spot.'

'And what about the dogs?'

'They both followed me. About a mile from the hut some blacks were camped. One gin was squatting at the fire, and I called her over, and gave her what I thought was Baines' dog, thinking it would get away from them and go back to the dray in the morning. It was dark, and in my flurry I made a mistake and gave her mine. When daylight came I found it out, but I could not drive the dog away, and it followed me home, for it remembered me. After hanging about, however, for a few days it disappeared, and, I suppose, made back to Boolah, where it was found. Everybody, of course, took it for my dog while it was here.'

'How did you come to know of the old track.'

'I did not know of it. I came on it by chance in the dark, and my horse followed it. As it was leading in the right direction I kept on until I came to the country I knew near Boolah.'

'And had some difficulty in getting your horse over the fence?' said Devine. 'Did it not strike you that giving the dog to the blacks would throw suspicion on them? I hope it was not done with that motive.'

'It was not,' she said eagerly; 'I made sure that the dog would get away, and I scarcely gave myself time to think. Afterwards, when it was too late, what you say occurred to me. Now I have told you everything. What I did was done almost in self-defence, and it was only what a father or brother would have done for me had I had one.'

She ceased and Devine was silent for a while. At last he spoke.

'Nobody has any suspicion of this but I. McFarlane saw the tracks, but I can easily put him off. The best thing to do is for Brown to ride back with me to Boolah and get your dog. For my part I shall hold my tongue and advise you to do the same.'

*   *   *

Now if the Malingerites had not quarrelled with the Layovahs, Devine and Bell would not have taken opposite sides in the affair. Devine would not have constituted himself an amateur detective, and the matter would have been left to the proper authorities, who might, possibly, have blundered on to the real culprit. As it is, the death of Baines, the hawker, has remained a mystery to all save one woman and one man.

THE HUT-KEEPER AND THE CATTLE-STEALER

SOME few years ago, ere the picturesque, grey, box-bark roofs on bush huts had given place to hard, ugly, angular galvanised iron; when real living shepherds were still in existence, and the stockmen who wore cabbage-tree hats, and made their own stockwhips instead of buying them from a store, had not all gone to the main camp, the following curious incident took place.

Alexander Macpherson, to give him his full name, was hut-keeping at a small outstation where, just at the period this story opens, he had only a couple of stockmen for companions. It was summer time; an iron drought had set in, and there was nothing to do but wait for rain and put off the mustering until more favourable weather. Under the circumstances, Sandy's two mates had got a few weeks' holiday and gone to the nearest town to spend it, that is, if they had succeeded in passing the first grogshanty—a matter of much doubt.

Sandy was noted as a careful soul who did not surrender himself to unrestrained joviality. He was reputed to have 'a stocking' somewhere, and was respected accordingly.

'Blessed if I'd stop here by myself for a week or two,' remarked Jim, the younger of the two, as he said good-bye on mounting.

'I don't see much in it,' returned Sandy; 'it's bound to be lonely, but I'll have my cheque in my pouch after all, and the publican will have yours.'

'But I'll have some fun, as well, old man; and you won't be lonely at this time of the year, if all they say's true,' was the reply.

'How's that? Who comes here?' demanded the hut-keeper.

'Some queer coves, according to all accounts, especially when they find a man alone'—and Jim waved his hand and cantered after his companion, leaving Sandy rather perplexed.

The out-station was twenty miles from the head-station. No other road led to it. To the West and North lay an unoccupied waste, and Sandy pondered over Jim's parting words without finding any clue to their meaning. In past days the blacks had been troublesome, but now they were all gone, so there was no harm to be apprehended from *them*.

Sandy turned into the hut and prepared for a fortnight's laziness. He had laid in a couple of bottles of whisky which, as he was a temperate man, would last him through the two weeks; he had the usual station luxuries, if he liked thus to enlarge his account, and the super, had sent him out a big bundle of old newspapers, so he felt equal to the occasion and dismissed his companion's words as idle.

Nothing happened in any way to disturb his serenity for ten days, and Sandy had by that time to acknowledge that solitude was a trifle monotonous. The summer night was moonless and dark, the mosquitoes were aggressive, and Sandy pricked up his slush-lamp, covered his fire over, and retired under the mosquito-net he had rigged round his bunk, taking with him a paper to read himself to sleep.

His eyelids were just commencing to grow heavy when he was aroused by the tramp of a horse. Then came the noise of a man dismounting, and before Sandy could get outside his carefully-tucked-in net, the door was opened and a stranger entered.

Sandy was a slow-going fellow who took things coolly; so he returned the stranger's greeting as a matter of course, and in the usual bush style made up the fire and put the billy on.

The new-comer was a silent man with a large red beard, and as he turned his head Sandy saw a livid weal or bruise encircling his neck.

After a few remarks intimating that he was a traveller wanting a night's shelter, he went out again, and Sandy heard him unsaddling and hobbling his horse; then he returned. He ate like a hungry man, but seemed to have an unaccountable difficulty in swallowing, and spoke little during his meal. Twice Sandy asked him where he came from without getting any reply, until on a third repetition, the newcomer told him curtly that that was no business of his, and a somewhat irksome silence ensued.

'You can take that bunk, mate,' said Sandy, stiffly, to break the spell, indicating the one belonging to the absent Jim.

'Thanks,' said the stranger; 'if you don't mind my keeping the fire going I'll sit up a bit—I don't feel sleepy.'

'Must be warm where you came from,' returned Sandy, 'when you want a fire such a night as this.'

'It *is* hot down there,' said the traveller, grimly.

Under cover of the mosquito-net Sandy lay and watched his taciturn guest. The man sat upon the rude slab bench, with his chin in his hands, gazing into the fire with an unwinking stare that made the watcher in the bunk feel that he should like very much to get up and seek some Dutch courage in a moderate dram. This could not be thought of, for he could scarcely infringe the laws of Australian hospitality so far as to drink without offering the other man anything.

So Sandy lay quiet, and was dropping off into a dose when a movement of the stranger aroused him.

The man had turned slightly, and the cook saw distinctly that little drops of blood were oozing from the discoloured bruise on his neck and running on to the collar of his shirt, where they merged into another and a deeper stain.

Sandy was horrified, and when the man presently arose, he almost gave a nervous start and cry, but he restrained himself. The stranger looked toward the darker portion of the hut, which was of some length, and shook his fist at a shadowy tie-beam just visible. Sandy's horror-stricken gaze followed in the same direction and—could he believe his eyes?—a rope with a noose at the end of it dangled from the beam!

60

'Get up, Sandy McPherson!' cried the visitor in a terrific voice, 'and don't lie shaking there any longer. I'm the man who hung himself here four years ago this night. Get up—I've got work for you!'

He made a stride as though to second his injunction, and Sandy with a quaking heart slipped out on to the earthen floor.

'Now, look here. To-morrow morning, sharp, you get a horse up and ride to Murderer's Camp—you know it—where all the niggers were shot, as you've heard tell of. I did most of that, and their black ghosts worried me till, at last, I up and hung myself. You go and watch on that camp all to-morrow until daylight next morning, and say a bit of a prayer for me, and mayhap I'll get some rest. If not—if you don't obey me—I'll haunt you, and hunt you, until you follow my example.' And he pointed with threatening finger to the shadowy beam and dangling noose.

The red-bearded man did not wait for any answer—in fact, Sandy could not have made one, his teeth chattered so. He watched his awful visitor open the door and close it after him; then he thought of the whisky. He got the bottle, took a deep draught without using a pannikin, and sank down on to his bunk half stupid and half asleep.

The sun was shining when he awoke, and he sprang up and looked about him. The rope and noose resolved itself into an ordinary halter thrown over the tie-beam, though Sandy could not for the life of him remember having seen it there before. There was certainly low tide in the whisky bottle, but he could not determine whether the bread and beef were in the same condition as before the stranger's visit.

His spirits fell, however, when he found the unmistakably fresh tracks of a horse outside the verandah. But if his visitor was a ghost, how did he come to ride a horse that made tracks? There could be no error, as he had swept all around the hut since the two men met. This thought struck Sandy very hard, and he sat down to work it out.

As a Highlander, Sandy was rather superstitious, but he had plenty of sense notwithstanding, and felt very sore at being caught unprepared and having shown the white feather. 'It's some lark of the fellows at the station,' he muttered to himself; 'going to make me spend a day out on Murderer's Camp and then "chiack" me about it. Not if I know it.'

Then a new thought struck him. The red-bearded man was certainly not one of the station men, nor from anywhere about. He was a stranger, and not anybody he knew in disguise; he had looked at him too well for that— no man can disguise his eyes. He knew the yarn of Murderer's Camp, and how men, gins, and piccaninies, had been ruthlessly slaughtered there; but he never heard of anyone committing suicide in the hut, and he began to doubt that there had been such an occurrence.

After referring for advice to the sadly-diminished whisky-bottle he made up his mind. He would go to Murderer's Camp—it was eight miles up the river. He would wait there until dark; then he would come back quietly and try to turn the tables.

Sandy had a horse of his own in the paddock. As a hut-keeper's horse should be, it was fat and fresh, and, with a supply of food, mental and otherwise, and an allowance of the second bottle of whisky—broached, alas! before its time—Sandy was soon on his way up the river.

Arrived at the Camp, he tied his horse up, for it was too fresh to trust in hobbles so near home. He then passed the day reading his newspapers and smoking. He kept his eyes about him, but could not say for certain that anyone was watching him, although at times his horse cocked its ears and whinnied suspiciously.

Night came on, and Sandy cautiously stole away, leading his horse and listening intently every now and then. But he heard nothing, and soon mounted and turned his willing steed homeward.

When within a mile or two of the hut, the familiar sound of cattle came to him on the faint wind. To a trained ear the noise made by cattle when freshly yarded is as distinct as possible from any sound they make when at large. 'Cattle in the yard!' thought Sandy; 'what's the matter?'

The stockyard was on his way, and he rode up to it. Although only hut-keeping, he had been too long on cattle-stations not to know the routine of the work.

The continued drought had deferred mustering so long that many of the unbranded calves were between six and twelve months old. At least two hundred cows with calves of the age mentioned had been yarded and drafted apart into different yards. The mothers were bewailing their lot at one end of the stockyard, and their children gnashing their teeth at the other.

Sandy grasped the situation at once; there was no room for doubt left. A raid had been made by a gang of cattle-duffers, and his absence had been desired in order that they might utilise the yard for drafting purposes; for, in spite of the tall 'blowing' of some bush hands, no one has ever yet, in a satisfactory manner, succeeded in drafting weaners from their mothers on a camp.

The men at the head station were idle, and he was supposed to be keeping watch on Murderer's Camp. He rode round the yard, thinking of these matters, amidst the furious bellowings going on, and then his attention was arrested by two things.

On the 'killing-gallows' hung a freshly-slaughtered beast, and in the yard immediately alongside were some ten or twelve horses.

More than that. As he ranged up alongside the rails in the clear moonlight, a head familiar to him was thrust through and exchanged friendly equine greetings with the horse he was riding.

He at once recognised the familiar front of Boomerang, the well-known racehorse belonging to the head station. Probably the others were also station horses, but it was too late to determine.

His first impulse was to throw down the slip-rails, let horses and cattle go, and then ride for his life, and had he done so he would have been saved a bitter experience. But his heart was full of rage at the manner in which he had been fooled, and he made up his mind to identify, at whatever personal risk, the men who had played the trick upon him.

He rode towards the hut, and, dismounting some distance off, crept cautiously up at the back and peered through the ill-fitting slabs.

A strong smell of fried steak proved that somebody had usurped his position. A party of five men were seated at the table, eating and drinking from the iron plates and tin pannikins he had so often cleaned. Listening, he heard their talk was of him. Redbeard was at the head of the table, and with much humour was describing his ghostly experience with Sandy the night before.

'I give you my word, boys, he's out at Murderer's Camp now, shaking in his shoes and praying that all hands and the cook up above will take pity on the soul of yours truly'

'How did you fix him?' said one.

'With a painted mark round my neck and my own devil's humour. It was the greatest fun out.'

Sandy listened with ears acock to the fullest extent, but shortly his attention was engaged by a man sitting opposite to the crack through which he was taking observation. The man's face was familiar to him. He had just served a sentence of ten years for cattle-stealing accompanied by armed violence. Sandy knew him before he was sentenced; knew him for the best rider in the district, and the most dreaded scoundrel. As he watched the lowering eyes and dogged, sullen manner, the man spoke:

'Now, boys! Time flies, and we must shape. That —— fool may be safe at Murderer's Camp or he may not; we don't know. Meantime, we must make sure. Two of you get up to the yard and let the weaners out, and steady them there as well as you can until we come, and catch our horses.'

Sandy's nerve betrayed him; he might have crept quietly off in the darkness under cover of the noisy bellowing going on at the yard, but he felt that the murderous eye of the black-muzzled ruffian opposite was on him, and that discovery meant death. In an instant the reins were over his horse's neck, his foot in the stirrup, and the next he was galloping for dear life over the flat.

Shouts, and a couple of shots, told him he had betrayed himself. The two men, whose horses were saddled, started in pursuit. Fortunately for Sandy, both he and his horse knew the bridle-track to the station, and his pursuers did not. One of them came to grief against a tree, and the other soon dropped behind, for the cook's horse was fresh, and, thanks to being tied up all day on the flat, in good fettle for a run.

Sandy galloped on three or four miles, and then pulled up to listen. Silence? No! the distant noise of a horse. A sudden conviction shot through Macpherson's mind, that it was the man he dreaded, mounted on Boomerang. He was lost! The horse was the fastest in the district, and the man who rode it a demon with a cat's eyes which could see on the darkest night, a man who could stick to anything that was ever foaled. The cook stuck the spurs in his nag and the race commenced. A deep sandy creek intervened about half way, and as he eased his horse over the shingle, under the gloomy sheoaks, it seemed to him that his enemy must be right on top of him, despite the long start he had got.

On, for another mile or two, and then Sandy thought his only chance was to turn and fight, for his game little horse showed signs of exhaustion, and took the spur without flinching. Suddenly he remembered that about six miles from the station there was a short cut across a rocky boulder-strewn hill. If he could turn off there, his pursuer might keep on the main track and miss him, so with eyes strained and heart beating he pushed on, while the clatter of Boomerang's hoofs drew nearer and nearer.

At last there was a turn in the road, and a dead tree that he knew; the short cut was close at hand, none too soon, for now the other horse was within two hundred yards. His horse knew the short cut as well as he did, and turned off of his own accord. Up the stony hill and down the other side, and then he pulled up and listened anxiously. His pursuer must have kept on. No! here he was close to him, and, with a mad, excited whinny, Boomerang dashed up to him—riderless.

Sandy felt like fainting for a moment, the tension had been so sharp, but he recovered himself and listened eagerly; save the hurried panting of the two horses the night was still as death. Boomerang had a saddle on, so he must have been ridden; but Sandy had no intention of enquiring after the fate of the rider at present, and, leading the racehorse, he made his way on to the station.

'For he's a jolly good fellow, for he's a jolly good fellow!' was the mocking chorus he heard as he approached the head station.

Some fun was evidently on the board, but his appearance and the tale he told soon stopped the festivity. There were fresh horses in the paddock, and a party was quickly on the way back.

'Hullo! what's up?' cried one, as the leader's horse shied suddenly near the junction of the short cut.

'There's a man on the road.'

Sandy's pursuer was lying there—with his neck broken. It had been a very near thing, after all. Boomerang had turned instinctively to follow the other horse along the short cut, his rider had pulled him off, and the racer had blundered and rolled over on the unfortunate man, who was the one Sandy had dreaded.

The cattle had been left in the yard, and only three station horses of not much value were missing. Suspicion lit on the owners of a small place, some seventy miles away, but nothing could be proved, and the red-bearded man had disappeared.

Years passed, and Macpherson had thriven. He was at Wagga once when a murder case was being tried, and made his way into the court just before the judge pronounced sentence. During the silence which followed the awful words Sandy, who was close up to the dock, turned to look at the prisoner. It was the ghost of the old hut! The hardened criminal recognised him too, and, with a grim and significant wink, put his hand to his neck, where the painted scar had been.

THE PARSON'S BLACKBOY

THE Rev. Joseph Simmondsen had been appointed by his bishop to a cure of souls in the Far North, in the days when Queensland was an ungodly and unsanctified place. Naturally, the Rev. J., who was young, green, and zealous, saw a direct mission in front of him. His predecessor had never gone twenty miles outside the little seaport that formed the commercial outlet of the district; but this did not suit Joseph's eager temperament. Once he felt his footing and gained a little experience, he determined on a lengthened tour that should embrace the uttermost limits of his fold.

Now, although beset with the conceit and priggishness inseparable from the early stages of parsonhood, Simmondsen was not a bad fellow, and glimpses of his manly nature would at times peep out in spite of himself. This, without his knowledge, ensured him a decent welcome, and he got a good distance inland under most favourable auspices, for, the weather being fine, everybody was willing to lend him a horse or drive him on to the next station upon his route. The Rev. Joseph began to think that the roughness of the back country had been much exaggerated.

In due course he arrived at a station which we will call Upton Downs; beyond it there were only a few newly-taken-up runs. On Upton Downs they were busy mustering, and when the parson enquired about his way for the next day the manager looked rather puzzled. 'You see,' he said, 'we are rather short-handed, and I can't spare a man to send with you; at the same time the track from here to Gundewarra is not very plain, and I am afraid you might not be able to follow it. However, I will see what I can do.'

Mr. Simmondsen was retiring to rest that night when a whispered conversation made itself audible in the next room. No words were distinguishable, but from the sounds of smothered laughter a good joke seemed to be in progress.

'I think I can manage for you,' said the superintendent at breakfast next morning. 'When you leave here you will go to Gundewarra, twenty-five miles. From there it is thirty-five miles to Bilton's Camp and ten on to Blue Grass. From Blue Grass you can come straight back here across the bush, about forty miles. I will lend you a blackboy who knows the country well and will see you round safely.'

The young clergyman thanked his host, and, after breakfast, prepared to leave. The blackboy, a good-looking little fellow arrayed in clean moles and twill shirt, was in attendance with a led pack-horse, and the two departed.

For some miles the Reverend Joseph improved the occasion by a little pious talk to the boy, who spoke fairly good English, and showed a white set of teeth when he laughed, as he constantly did at everything the parson said. At midday they camped for an hour on the bank of a lagoon, in which Mr. Simmondsen had a refreshing swim. In the evening they arrived at their destination, and received the usual welcome.

'I see you adapt yourself to the customs of the country,' said his host at mealtime, and a slight titter went round the table. The Reverend Joseph joined in, taking it for granted that his somewhat unclerical garb was alluded to. In reply to enquiries he was informed that Bilton's Camp was a rough place, and Blue Grass even worse; and he was pleased to hear it, for up to now his path had been too pleasant altogether; he hadn't had a chance to reprove anybody.

Bilton's Camp proved to be indeed a rough place. The men were civil, however, and as the parson had had another exhilarating bath at the midday camp he appreciated the rude fare set before him, although here, as at the other place, there seemed to be a joke floating about that made everybody snigger.

The next day's journey, to Blue Grass, was but a short stage, and as the reverend gentleman had by this time become very friendly with Charley, the blackboy, the two rode along chatting pleasantly until they came somewhat unexpectedly on the new camp.

A very greasy cook and two or three gins in dilapidated shirts were the only people at home, and they stood open-eyed to greet the stranger.

Although Mr. Simmondsen had suited his attire to his surroundings, he still retained enough of the clerical garb to signify his profession. The cook, therefore, at once took in the situation, and invited the parson under the tarpaulin which did temporary duty as a hut.

He informed his visitor, at whom he looked rather curiously, that 'everyone' was away, camped out, and that no one would return for a couple of days; that he was alone, excepting for two men who were at work in a yard a short distance off, and who would be in to dinner; in fact, they came up while he was speaking. Mr. Simmondsen took great interest in this, the first real 'outside' camp he had seen, and as the two bushmen had gone down to the creek for a wash, and the cook was busy preparing a meal, he called Charley to ask him a few questions.

'What are these black women doing about the place, Charley?'

'O! all about missus belongah whitefellow,' was the astonishing reply.

It was some moments before Joseph could grasp the full sense of this communication; then he considered it his duty to read these sinners a severe lecture, and prepared one accordingly.

'Do you not understand,' he said, when the three men were together, 'the trespass you are committing against both social and Divine laws? If you do not respect one, perhaps you will the other.'

The cook stared at the bushmen in blank amazement, and the bushmen at the cook.

'I allude to these unfortunate and misled beings,' said the parson, waving his hand towards the half-clad gins.

A roar of laughter was the reply. 'Blessed if that doesn't come well from *you!*' said the cook, when he could speak. The others chuckled in acquiescence.

'What do you mean?' said the indignant Joseph; 'I speak by right of my office.'

'Sit down and have some tucker,' said the cook, 'you're not a bad sort, I can see, but don't come the blooming innercent.'

The indignant pastor refused. He saw that his words were treated lightly, that no one would listen to him, and he left in high dudgeon. Charley had told him that there was a good lagoon about twelve miles on the road back to Upton Downs; he would go on there and camp—they had plenty of provisions on the pack-horse—and taking his bridle and calling the boy he went to catch his horse.

As he came back he overheard the fag-end of a remark the cook was making to the others. 'They came round the end of the scrub chatting as thick as thieves, and when I seed who it was—Lord! you could have wiped me out with one hand.'

This was worse than Greek to the Reverend. Greek he might have understood. In spite of a clumsy apology from the delinquent, he departed, and near sundown arrived at the lagoon Charley had spoken of. It was a lovely spot. One end was thick with broad-leaved water-lilies, but there was a clear patch at the other end promising the swim the good parson enjoyed so much.

When the tent was pitched he stood in Nature's garb about to enter the water, when Charley called to him. Pointing towards the lilies he told Mr. Simmondsen that he would get him some seed-pods which the blacks thought splendid eating. The clergyman had only got up to his waist before he heard a plunge behind him and saw Charley's dark form half-splashing, half-swimming towards the lilies. Presently his head emerged from a dive, and he beckoned towards the clergyman to come over and taste the aboriginal luxury. The Reverend paddled lazily over and investigated. The seed-pods proved of very pleasant flavour, and as the sun was nearly down, Mr. Simmondsen wended his way to the bank and emerged in the shallow water, with Charley a few paces behind him. For some reason he looked back. Shocking predicament! There was no shirking the fact: all the quiet laughter about 'the customs of the country,' the unexplained allusions, the ribald manner of the cook, were evident at a flash. Charley was a woman!

The wicked superintendent of Upton Downs had started him on his travels with ('after the customs of the country') a black gin dressed in boy's clothes as a valet, and that gin had evidently been recognised by everyone on the road. Mr. Simmondsen thought of the past and blushed. That night was spent in fervent prayer.

*   *   *

'My dear sir,' said Davis, the super. of Upton Downs, 'I did the best I could for you. Charlotte is as good as any blackboy and knows all the country round here. Now, own up, did not she look after you well?'

'You forget the scandal that may arise,' said the Reverend Mr. Simmondsen.

'Lord, man! who cares about what is done out here? Nobody will ever hear of it.'

*   *   *

Davis was wrong. Everybody did hear of it. The Reverend Mr. Simmondsen received indignant letters from his Bishop, his churchwardens, the Reverend Mr. Wriggle, the West Australian Missionary, several missionary societies, and, last and worst, a letter of eternal farewell from the young lady to whom he was engaged. Fortunately he inherited some money at the time; so he did the best thing possible—threw up the church, went into squatting, and is now one of the most popular men in the district.

A LUCKY MEETING

I.

'WHAT do you make of it, Jim?'

'Looks remarkably like an E, but what can be the meaning of the extraordinary triangular thing that follows?'

'That's the puzzle. The first mark one could swear had been made by a white man; but the other is apparently one of those queer carvings which the blacks make. There, however, is the scar plain enough, where the bark was stripped, and from the shape of the piece removed I think it's like a white man's work.'

'Moreover,' added Jim, 'it has been done with a steel tomahawk.'

The two men were standing in front of a dead coolibah tree of some size, on which the marks they were trying to decipher had been deeply cut. It was the shore of a broad, shallow lake surrounded by a forest of similar dead trees—white skeletons, lifting heavenwards their writhing, bare limbs. A stranger, set down there suddenly would say that the axe of the ring-barker had been at work; but the locality was away in the far interior, where the white man had only just intruded on the solitude. Round the lake, which at its deepest only averaged a few feet, was a border of green, luscious grass; back from that ring of verdure reigned desolation and sterility.

Loose, puffy soil, broken into mounds and hollows, seamed with gaping cracks. On these dusty mounds were heaped thousands of tiny shells; in the hollows drooped a few withered stalks of nardoo. On all sides the gaunt, lifeless trees. Two exceptionally wet years had, in some remote time, deluged the plain, and the long-standing, stagnant water destroyed the timber.

This state of things is not uncommon in many parts of the North Australian interior. In the deepest hollows of these dry lake-beds lie the bones of fish, which have escaped their feathered enemies, to perish slowly as their native element evaporated. On the broader expanse, bleached skeletons are mouldering; the grotesque-headed pelican and the dingo, with a wild-dog snarl on his fleshless jaws. Bird and beast have made for the lake after long, long flight, and hot, dusty tramp, only to find there drought, disappointment and death. To the north-west, where a bank has been formed by the action of the steady south-east monsoon, layer after layer of dead shells has been deposited by the constantly-lapping wavelets, weak forms of life that have lived and died in the waters of the ephemeral lake. Beyond and around these depressions wherein the overflow of a rarely heavy rainfall accumulates, are the great plains whose treeless edges meet the sky in an unbroken straight line. Where the tall columns of dust revolve in a wild waltz; where, in summer time, the air is so aglow with heat that it throbs like a living thing, and in this fierce atmosphere is born the treacherous mirage: a bush becomes a tree, a stone a rock, and the hard, baked clay-pan a blue lakelet. This is riverless Australia, the sun-god's realm, the region of short-lived creeks, lost for ever in these dead, dry lake-beds.

The elder of the brothers who had been regarding the tree copied the inscription in his note-book, and the two strolled back to their camp where a blackboy was watching the boiling of a piece of dried beef. They sat down and commenced smoking.

'How long do you suppose these trees have been dead?' said Sam Gilmore, the elder of the two.

'Impossible to say, for certain, but about ten or fifteen years.'

'Yes,' returned Sam, after some silent puffs, 'that would be about it. There was a devil of a wet season all over the north in '72 and '73. That mark was made before then, when the tree was alive.'

'Certainly it was, and if you remember the Herbert was settled in the sixties. Some fellow from the tableland has been out here, that's about all it is.'

Sam looked at his note-book. 'I've got it!' he exclaimed. '"E. triangle". It's a station-brand. Many fellows have a trick of cutting their brand on a tree instead of their initials.'

'That will be it,' replied his brother, 'there were no registered brands, all of one pattern, in those days.'

The two thought little more about the matter, but were busily employed the next two days in examining the surrounding country, it being part of a large block they had taken up in the Northern Territory. One evening the blackboy, who had been left in camp to look after the spare horses and see that they did not get bogged, remarked with the laconic suddenness of the aboriginals: 'Old man horse sit down,' indicating by a motion of his hand the far side of the lake.

'Which one horse?' said Sam, thinking he meant that one of their own had got bogged.

'Baal mine know. Long time that fellow sit down. Old man bone.'

'A skeleton of a horse?' queried Jim, looking at his brother.

Sam nodded. 'We will have a look at it to-morrow—too late to go all round there this evening.'

Next morning, guided by the blackboy, they were soon beside the bones of the animal, which lay in a patch of grass, almost concealed from view. Evidently the moist border of the lake had saved them from destruction by the bush fires that annually swept the surrounding country.

'A horse, but how the deceased came here, there is no evidence to show,' said Jim.

The blackboy was poking about with a stick. 'That fellow bin carry saddle,' and from the mouldering rubbish he dragged out the corroded iron-work.

Inspired by this discovery a closer search was made. The plated buckles of a saddlepouch were found, a plated sandwich-case, such as hunting-men carry in England, and the blade of a large pocket-knife. Everything in the shape of leather had long vanished.

They devoted all the morning to examining the vicinity, but no further relics were forthcoming, and, taking what they had found with them, the brothers returned to camp.

During the afternoon Sam set to work cleaning the old sandwich-case. By dint of hard rubbing he succeeded in restoring it to something like cleanliness, and although time and exposure had dealt hardly with the metal, a monogram became faintly visible on one side, and on the other was roughly scratched the mark they had found on the tree, 'E and a triangle.'

'Now,' said Jim, after the examination, 'let's have a look at the inside.' He inserted the point of his knife beneath the half-cover and, after some trouble, raised it. Inside were some papers, loose sheets, torn from a note-book, on which the pencil-writing was faint and illegible; but there was a larger sheet of blue letter-paper, on which the writing was in ink and, although slightly yellow, plain and distinct. The battered old case had been true to its trust and, despite all, had preserved the message confided to it.

The brothers perused their strange find and, at the conclusion, looked at each other in silence for a few moments.

'This is a strange document to drop across in such a howling wilderness,' said Sam at length.

Jim whistled in sympathy. 'I suppose,' he remarked, 'the writer came to grief, and his horse made back to the water, got bogged and died. Is that how you read it?'

'I think so. At any rate, it's too long ago for us to bother looking up tracks. The date on this—December 4th, 1870—coincides with the time we surmised.'

'I suppose you'll keep it?' queried Jim.

'Most carefully. It belongs to the man's children, and may be valuable, or, perhaps, only waste paper. Possibly we shall find out when we get back to civilisation; meanwhile I vote we make a start for home tomorrow. We are satisfied, I suppose, that this country is good enough.'

'All right,' said the younger; and for the rest of the day they devoted themselves to preparations for an early departure on the morrow, dismissing the subject of their strange discovery from their minds.

II.

Young Simpson propped himself up against the slabs and gazed disconsolately down the sunny road. He was suffering a bad recovery, his pockets were empty, and his credit exhausted. He had lately finished a job of horse-breaking, and had knocked his cheque down in orthodox style. Now, life was all dust and ashes, and everything a mockery and a delusion. He was only thirty-six, and had already managed to break every breakable bone in his body, and pull through several bad attacks of *delirium tremens.* He was the son of a well-to-do squatter, but ere he was twenty had managed to incense his father so bitterly that he had been cast forth without even the proverbial shilling, and a younger brother, a good and well-behaved youth, reigned in his stead. Since his expulsion from home he had steadily gone to the dogs, and it was a pity, for, however weak, he was a good-hearted young fellow. A strong, helping hand would have saved him, but he never got it, and now it was too late. At least so everybody thought and said.

Simpson had been dozing on a rude bench in the verandah, and had just got on to his feet, under the impression that somebody had ridden up and aroused him. Presumably this impression was correct, for a horse was hitched up to the rail outside, and voices could be heard in the bar. Possibly there was a drink on hand. He licked his dry lips with a still dryer tongue, and lurched inside.

A deeply sun-tanned man, with bright eyes, was talking to the landlord.

'Here, Joe,' said the latter to Simpson, 'come and have a wet, you look sleepy.'

This was most astonishing; only that morning his credit had been peremptorily stopped, and now he was invited to refresh himself. The landlord shifted down the bar a bit and Simpson followed him.

'This gent,' said the publican in a subdued tone, 'has got a mob of cattle going north, and wants another hand badly. I'll put in a good word for you, and, perhaps, he'll be right for a bit of an advance, so that you can square up with me before you go.'

Simpson 'dropped' to the situation at once. He immediately poured out a drink so 'long' that it made the landlord eager to clutch the bottle again. Refreshed by this, he accosted the stranger, and with few words a bargain was struck, and Joe Simpson went off to roll up his scanty belongings in his blanket.

'As good a man as ever crossed a horse,' said the effusive publican; 'only keep him off the booze. Born a gentleman, too.'

Jim Gilmore, for it was he, on his way out with cattle to stock the country he and his brother had lately examined, looked curiously after the retreating form. He was warm-hearted, and something in the ne'er-do-well had appealed to him.

*   *   *

The long trip drew to an end, and tired men, leg-weary horses, and listless cattle all desired the arrival of that morning when they should mutually take leave of each other. Dry stages had been successfully crossed, wet, blustering nights experienced, and death in many forms had taken toll of the herd before Jim, with a sigh of relief, dismounted on the bank of a long serpentine lagoon, some twenty miles from the shallow lake where they had formerly camped. Leaning on his horse he watched the long string of cattle troop in to the water.

'Poor Joe!' he thought, as he caught sight of Simpson steadying the leaders, 'he's got a bad touch of this northern fever. Glad we are here so that he can get a spell.'

The blatant publican's recommendation had turned out true. A better man than Joe Simpson had proved himself could scarce be found. Ever ready when the weather was bad and the cattle rowdy on camp; always alert during the long sleepless nights across the dry plains, and alas! never neglecting the opportunity of a short spree in the few townships they had passed, Joe had been young Gilmore's right hand throughout the tedious journey. Now, the malarial fever that the cattle seem to turn up with their hoofs from the virgin soil in new country had recognised his ill-used constitution and seized on him.

The day after the herd was turned out Joe lay delirious under a bough shade.

Jim devoted all his spare time to him, and at last had the satisfaction of witnessing his return to reason. But Simpson was very weak—he had played too many tricks with his physique to be able to stand a severe attack of fever with impunity, and lay almost apathetic as regarded his chances of final recovery.

One morning Jim noticed that the patient had been idly tracing letters and signs on the dusty earth alongside his rude bed of dry grass. Amongst them he recognised with a start the E followed by a triangle.

'What are you up to, Joe?' he said quietly.

'Just trying to remember a lot of brands,' returned Simpson, in his weak voice.

'Whose brand is that?' asked Gilmore, indicating the one he was interested in.

Simpson's wasted face flushed hotly. 'When a fellow gets down in the world,' he said, after a pause, 'he does not always stick to his right name. That brand was our old station brand on my father's place. There were three partners at first, Emerson, Unthorpe, and Charters, and, as their initials made the first syllable of Euclid, they took the triangle as a brand with my father's initial before it. Finally he bought them out, and my brother has the place now.'

'Then,' said Jim, staring hard at him, 'your name is—?'

'Emerson.'

'Good God!'

'What is the matter? What do you know about me?' cried the invalid anxiously.

'Nothing, nothing, go on. Tell me, where did your father die? How is it you were left so badly off?'

Joe Emerson looked at his questioner with some surprise, but answered quietly enough. 'My father died in his bed on Bellbrook station, where I was born. He and I had quarrelled some years before and finally he disowned me. I was a bad lot, there's no denying.'

'Was your father ever up this way?'

'Yes. He had a share in a station in the north of Queensland, and took a trip out west, I know. In fact, it was through some terrible hardship he endured that he afterwards died. He was too old to stand it. I never heard the rights of it, but I believe through some stupid blunder of one of the men some of their horses got away from them on a dry stage with packs and saddles on. My father and the others managed to get into water, but the horses made back and probably perished.'

'Your brother then took your place in your father's will, and you were left out in the cold. Do you know the date of that will?'

'It was the time of our final row, in the beginning of '69.'

Jim strode outside and thought for a moment, then he returned. 'This is the strangest thing I ever came across outside of a novel. I have good news for you. Your father must have been in a tight place before the horses were lost, and when he anticipated death he repented of his harshness to you, and wrote out another will. It commences: "I, George Henry Emerson, now expecting death, and being desirous of making amends to my dear son Joseph for my stern conduct." I do not remember any more, but it was duly witnessed by Isaac Wright and Thomas Peberdy. Do you know anything about them?'

Young Emerson was looking at Jim as though bewildered by what he heard, and answered slowly. 'Peberdy was an old servant of my father's, and went north with him; he has a selection now, down south. Wright I don't know. But surely you remember the purport of this will?'

'Certainly. It left the whole of his property to you, subject to certain charges on it for your brother and sister.'

'But—but, Mr. Gilmore!' cried the sick man, impatiently, 'how did you find it? Who has it now?'

'My brother has it now. We found it with the remains of your father's horse, preserved in an old-fashioned sandwich case. Do you remember it?'

'Yes, with his monogram on it; he brought it from England.'

'If the two witnesses are alive, it seems to me that the will cannot be disputed. My brother may be here at any time; he knows when we are due, and is bringing up supplies from Burketown, and will probably push ahead.'

There was silence for a short time; then Emerson reached out and felt for Gilmore's hand. He grasped it and sat upright. 'Look here,' he said, 'I'm going to do three things.'

'Don't be in a hurry,' murmured Jim.

'I'm going to get well.'

'Hear, hear!'

'I'm going to knock off liquor.'

'Hear, hear, hear!' from Gilmore.

'And I'm going to get the skeleton of that old horse set up and mounted on a pedestal.'

'When the will is proved, I presume,' said his companion.

No need to tell much more. One witness was alive and able to swear to the signatures. Joe kept to his three resolutions. The skeleton of the old horse adorns the hall of Bellbrook station, and Jim Gilmore's wife was once Miss Emerson.

THAT OTHER FELLOW: A TALE OF THE SEVENTIES

DUNCAN MCINTYNE sat on the cap of the stockyard-fence, smoking quietly, contemplating a colt which, in his capacity of horse-breaker, he was about to mount for the first time. The colt was also contemplating Duncan, and wondering what fresh devilry he meditated. Only a week ago and he was as free as air; now he was penned in by posts and rails, his mouth sore with a breaking-bit, a roller had been buckled around him, in which he felt as comfortable as a girl in her first corset, his mane and tail had been pulled, and to-day a saddle had been girthed on him—all these indignities he justly attributed to the man 'cockatooing' on the fence. He had been violently taking it out of himself bucking round the yard, and now stood breathlessly gazing at his enemy.

Duncan knocked the ashes out of his pipe, replaced it in his pouch, and sprang lightly down into the enclosure. A blackfellow, who had been sunning himself in a corner, arose also on noticing the movement. Between fear and exertion the colt was sweating profusely, the perspiration dropped from his body on to the dusty ground, and ran in dirty streams down his legs. After a smart display of equine temper, Duncan got his hand on the youngster's mane and spoke soothingly to him.

'Steady, old boy, you've had your fling like the rest of us, and now work begins.'

The pair looked in each other's eyes like two duellists. Neither man nor horse could foresee the future; there they were on an equality of ignorance. No instinct could tell the animal that a time would come when he would appeal to his hated foe with piteous whinnies for relief, and die with that hand caressing him, and those eyes full of unshed tears for his fate.

The blackboy approached the horse's head while Duncan made his usual preparations to mount. 'My word!' said the boy as he got hold of the colt's ear, 'this the fellow Sherman Jarley say, kick out mid his front feet that time we brand him.'

'Yes, Billy,' returned Duncan, flipping the stirrup-leather once or twice against the flap of the saddle; 'and if you don't let go quick he'll shake hands with you as he did with German Charley. Now!'

With a quick, easy movement he was in the saddle, and the boy stepped back. For a moment the colt stood motionless, then started pawing and rearing, and again stood doggedly still.

'Now don't sulk,' said McIntyre, but the words were no sooner uttered than the colt started bucking in a vicious and roundabout fashion, which called upon all the rider's powers of horsemanship. The struggle lasted a short time only, and then the horse gave in defeated.

'Get your horse, Billy,' says McIntyre, and the boy, after letting down the rails, mounts an old horse which has been standing indifferent and half-asleep in an adjacent yard; then the colt, after a little coaxing, goes off quietly down the paddock alongside the old stager.

Duncan McIntyre was a gentleman who had gone down in the world. He was one of the curst victims of heredity; only, unfortunately for himself, he had not succeeded to the whisky-proof head of his Scottish ancestors. Liquor ever turned him from a generous, easy-going, mild-tempered fellow into a mad rowdy, ready to ride a wild race through the main street of a bush township, fight with his best friend, or drink with his worst enemy. Fortunately, his manly, adventurous character had prevented him sinking into the ranks of the sponger and the loafer. He had fallen from his own set to an ordinary bush-hand, and could always earn a good cheque at any kind of work, but this was surely followed by the fatal and inevitable 'spree.' Some morning he would awake possessed of nothing but the clothes he had slept in, 'a liver' a blue-blanket and a bottle of 'sudden death,' kindly given him by the publican to stave off the impending 'horrors.'

One day Fate led him to Darromine, a medium-sized cattle-station. Mitford, the managing partner, was a man gifted with an exceptionally good and kindly heart. He knew McIntyre's story, soon recognised the worth dormant beneath the assumed roughness of the fallen nature, and, after some trouble, induced him to come and live with him, and endeavour to assume once more the habits of his better days. Naturally, the besetting sin betrayed itself from time to time, but Mitford set himself to banish the unclean spirit, and by untiring vigilance, unaccompanied by any ostentatious display of solicitude, he partly succeeded. Needless to say that Duncan had conceived a strong and lasting friendship for the other.

II.

Some fifteen miles from Darromine there was a small township, and in that township lived the fair and only daughter of the police-magistrate thereof, a widower. She was nineteen and the belle of the district. Not that she prided herself on that distinguished position, for there were only five girls in the district, all told, and the other four were so uncommonly hard-featured that to be the acknowledged belle in such company was, after all, but a doubtful distinction. Doubtless Miss Jennie Webster cherished a hidden conviction, in which she was quite justified, that, had she to compete with more favoured rivals she would have held her own; but this notion she kept to herself, and did not assume any undue airs as the belle of Corraville. Needless to say that all the youths of the district were madly in love with her, even those who professed engagements with absent fair ones in Sydney or Melbourne. Jennie smiled upon all alike, but favoured no one in particular.

Now it happened that the very day on which Duncan gave the colt his first lesson had been selected by Mr. Webster to drive his daughter to Darromine on a visit. McIntyre and Billy were walking the horses quietly homeward along the Corraville road, which led through the paddock, when at a turn amongst some scrub they were suddenly overtaken by the buggy. The colt shied violently and commenced to buck. It was rather awkward in the scrub, and Duncan was nearly getting into trouble two or three times ere he brought his green mount under control. After offering his apologies for unintentionally frightening the colt, which the young lady accepted with a frank smile of admiration, for most women like to see good horsemanship, the police-magistrate and his daughter drove on.

'What a quiet man that Mr. McIntyre is,' said Jennie, 'I can never get half-a-dozen words out of him; but he *can* ride.'

Her father smiled somewhat grimly; McIntyre's past was known to him, and he was glad to see the change that was being worked.

'It's a case of still waters, my girl,' he replied, 'but he is a good fellow, I believe.'

Mitford was one of Jennie's victims. For a long time he had been ready to lay himself and his share of Darromine at her feet; the present visit, therefore, translated him to the seventh heaven.

'How well you ride, Mr. McIntyre!' said Miss Webster in the course of the dinner. 'I must confess I like to see a bit of good buckjumping.'

Duncan smiled. 'I nearly came to grief under that low brigalow though,' he said.

'I saw it,' she returned; 'and I can assure you my heart was in my mouth, for it was all our fault.'

'How does he shape?' asked Mitford, alluding to the colt.

'Very well indeed. I have taken a great fancy to him, he has no vice—it's only nervousness. In a week he'll get confidence, and in a month I'll make a lady's hack of him.'

'There! Miss Webster,' said Mitford; 'may I send him in for you to ride this day month if McIntyre guarantees that he is fit?'

'Certainly, I accept the challenge,' she returned, for she was a good horsewoman. 'I will rely upon Mr. McIntyre's skill and judgment.'

Duncan bowed and the subject dropped; but thenceforth the colt, christened Challenger, became the object of special care and attention.

The month passed, and Miss Webster, arrayed in a workmanlike habit of dark blue serge, was seated in the verandah reading a book, and occasionally glancing along the road which led to Darromine. A rider with a led horse presently made his appearance, but, sooth to say, the young lady looked slightly disappointed. 'He might have come too, to see how the colt went,' she thought.

'Are you ready, dad?' she called out; 'here comes Mr. Mitford with the horse.'

Mitford rode into the stable yard, and the magistrate and his daughter came out to inspect the colt. What a difference to the sullen, fierce-eyed rebel who had snorted defiance at his enemy only thirty days before!

'Oh, dad, isn't he a beauty!' cried the little lady in her delight.

'McIntyre has handled him so that a child could ride him, but he is full of pluck all the same,' said Mitford, delighted at her pleasure.

Challenger was soon saddled, and the three set out; the trim-figured Jennie forgetting her annoyance at the non-appearance of McIntyre in the pleasure of her mount. The ride was a success, and thenceforth Challenger was entirely at Miss Webster's disposal.

It is impossible for a girl and a man to be on the verge of a violent passion for each other without both knowing it, although never a word may have been interchanged on the subject. Jennie had not quite suffered herself to fall in love with the interesting Duncan, but she was perilously near it. McIntyre himself was lost. He had fought against the feeling tooth and nail; had told himself over and over again that the curse which shadowed his life made it a heinous crime for him to think of marriage; and had almost won the fight. Suddenly the fatal knowledge came to him that it needed but a word from him to obtain the confession of her affection. The flower was unfolding for him to pluck. He almost threw caution to the winds. Almost—not quite.

Mitford came back from Corraville one evening with his sunny face clouded: he had ventured all, and lost.

'I am sure she would have had me, old man,' he innocently confided to his friend, 'but there's another fellow in the way; she as good as admitted it.'

Duncan was silent for some time; then he rallied his companion, and somewhat roused him from his despondency.

'Look here, McIntyre,' said Mitford, 'I have a plan in my head about which I have already consulted my partner and obtained his consent. You have heard of the country out west beyond the Queensland border? We are thinking of taking a bit up, and sending out some of our spare stock to form for us a station. Will you go out and manage for a third share and a salary?'

Duncan rose and shook the other's hand. 'Your offer is too generous. You could get a man anywhere for a couple or three hundred a year.'

'No, we couldn't, not such an all-round man as you. Besides, it's not all beer and skittles living out there. What with fever and blacks and short commons, you'll earn your third share.'

'When do you propose to start?'

'You and I and a blackboy will go as soon as possible and inspect the country. When we come back we will start the cattle, provided we find anything good enough. We have three years' grace to stock.'

'There is nothing much to do here,' returned McIntyre, 'we can start in a fortnight.' After a few more words they parted for the night. McIntyre lay sleepless, thinking of what the day had brought forth. She might have accepted Mitford, but for that other fellow. He, Duncan McIntyre, the ne'er-do-well, was 'that other fellow.' His way was clear: before him lay escape from the temptation of love, and perhaps a drunkard's death; he must go, and go quickly without speaking.

Of a sudden he asked himself would she forget him? Would not his exile in the wilderness arouse the very flame he sought to extinguish, by adding the touch of absence and romance? No, that other fellow must go under in a way that would conclude the matter. Mitford on his return would probably get a favourable answer. 'That other fellow' went under that night, although Mitford on his restless bed little thought so.

McIntyre had broken out again. That was the last news in the little township where news was so scarce. Everybody said they had expected it all along, and everybody, saving the local publicans, said they were very sorry. It had been 'an old man spree.' Duncan had damaged the sergeant of police, who was good-naturedly trying to induce him to leave town. Mitford had to come in and bail him out of the lock-up. Jennie had heard of it, and shed some bitter tears but, with all a woman's faith in the reforming power of love, still believed that had she the right she could exorcise the evil spirit. Alas for Jennie! the worst was yet to come.

McIntyre went 'on the tear' again, and this time capped all his former delinquencies. One of the publicans had imported a new barmaid, a young damsel with gold-washed hair, who rejoiced in the name of Flossie. Duncan rode Challenger into town, and an hour or two afterwards Flossie might have been seen steering the colt down the main street in the sight of all people. Jennie saw her, saw this garish young party mounted on the horse that had been kept sacred to her use, that McIntyre had devoted weeks to breaking in for her—Challenger, her pet who ate sugar from her hand!

From that moment poor Duncan was to her a thing of the most bitter scorn and contempt. He might have damaged the whole of the police-force and painted the town scarlet, and been forgiven; but this insult was too much. That other fellow went under for good and all.

One small bit of triumph was afforded her. The vainglorious Flossie, flushed with the pride that precedes a fall, took opportunity, when parading before the P.M.'s house, to give Challenger a cruel and undeserved cut across the ears. This for a horse of spirit, accustomed to be treated as a gentleman, was unendurable. Already irritated by the antics of his strange rider, he gave a side-bound that seated Flossie, to her sudden astonishment, in the middle of the dusty road. Challenger trotted off, and the forlorn damsel, holding up her skirt, had to follow on foot, amidst much chaff from the spectators.

Mitford got McIntyre out of town, somehow. Hurt as he was he refrained from reproach, and he was rewarded. Ere they started, he asked once more, and this time he was told, 'When you come back I may say yes.' What more would he have?

Once only did Jennie allude to the disgraceful episode. 'I hope you are taking that horse with you, I never want to see him again.' Mitford assured her that the innocent animal which had done its best to protest against indignity, would never more be seen by her, little dreaming of a time to come when life and hope would be bound up in Challenger's endurance and his rider's faith.

They parted, and Jennie, watching, saw another horseman join him in the main street, and she turned into the house with a bright sparkle in her eye and a flush upon her cheek.

III.

A wide stretch of grey plain, bounded by a shimmering haze, a haze that grotesquely magnifies what few objects are visible, turning a stone into a rock, a bush into a tree. A shallow depression, bordered by dry polygonum bushes, with here and there a crooked, distorted coolibah tree, threads this plain. At one point in this apology for a creek, there is a pool of milky looking water. From the edge of this pool a short growth of green grass extends for a little distance up the bank, and on this patch of sward, the only green thing visible, some horses are feeding. Under a scanty shade of boughs, erected near one of the largest coolibah trees, Mitford and McIntyre are sitting; blackened by sun and wind, thin with semi-starvation, and cursed with 'the infinite torment of flies.' The blackboy is curled up under the trunk of the tree. He lets the flies cluster around his eyes, infest his mouth and nostrils, and makes no effort, like the white men, to drive them away. The others are less patient, and a hasty exclamation continually escapes them. 'When shall we get out of this purgatory?' says Mitford.

They were in a trap. They had penetrated far into the unknown country west of the Queensland border. From one scanty water-hole to another they had made their way to their present position, and now they could neither advance nor retreat. Before them there was an illimitable expanse of dry country; behind them the water-holes had dried up, and their return was cut off. Sturt, at the Depôt Camp, was in the same fix, and scores of men since have been caught in a similar way. A hundred and twenty miles of dry, cracked, gaping plains lay between them and a large permanent lagoon they had found on their outward journey. No horse could travel that distance without water under the vertical summer sun. No horse could traverse half the distance over the soft, spongy soil full of holes and deep cracks and live. Their only hope was a kindly thunderstorm, for the water-hole where they were camped was fast shrinking, and when that was gone it meant death.

Day after day they watched the clouds gather, dark and threatening, only to break in wind and dust, and a few fierce flashes of lightning.

At last, an ominous cloud gathered in the east. As night drew on, the heavens darkened and the setting sun was reflected from the opposite hemisphere in a quickly-fading flush of angry scarlet. A black night closed in. The air was heavy, oppressive and sultry; the two men and the boy stood silently watching. Their fate was hidden in that sullen bank of vapour. Quick, bright flashes of lightning soon commenced to blaze, followed, after a long interval, by a low, distant mutter of thunder. Presently even this ceased, and, with a sigh of bitter disappointment, the men stretched themselves on their blankets and sought forgetfulness in sleep.

'How far off was that storm?' said Mitford, breaking the silence.

'Any distance over seventy miles,' returned Duncan. 'Did you not notice the long interval between the flash and the thunder?'

Mitford replied wearily, and both men soon slept.

In an hour or two McIntyre awoke, and instantly noticed a change in the atmosphere. The wind was blowing faintly from the direction of the late storm, and with it came the unmistakeable smell of wet earth. Rain had fallen to the eastward at last. The wind had brought the message, but from how far had it come?

Duncan aroused Mitford, and together they stood and sniffed the cool, damp air.

'We must get out of here somehow,' said McIntyre at last. 'Now, listen. I am going to take Challenger and a pack-horse with water, and ride in the direction that wind comes from; I have the bearing, a little south of east. I will let the packhorse go in about twenty miles, after I have given Challenger a drink from the bags; the pack-horse will come back here. I shall go on until I find where that storm fell. If I don't come back you will know it is too far, and that I am done for; then you must shift for yourself. If I find water I shall come back.'

'But, Duncan, what nonsense! Why can't we all go and chance it?'

'Because I might get a little puddle of water that would serve me and the horse and would not be enough for all of us. Man, don't you understand! I owe you a debt and must pay you in my own way. For God's sake, don't thwart me.'

Mitford could say no more. McIntyre roused up Billy, and they strode into the darkness after the horses, which were soon caught, and, under the now starlit sky, the two men said good-bye.

About three hours after daylight, McIntyre pulled up, watered Challenger by means of a tin dish he had on the pack, then released the pack-horse to find its own way back to camp, and proceeded on his lonely way. Hour after hour of monotonous progress over the dead, dry plain, the only break an occasional shallow depression bordered with brown polygonum. Hour after hour through the great stillness of the night, save for a short occasional rest for his gallant horse.

Daylight again, and the outlook unchanged—no sign of rainfall visible. As the sun got hotter Challenger began to show signs of distress, so Duncan started to walk, and together man and horse stumbled over the treacherous plain. He had a small canvas bag of water on his saddle, but only a scanty remnant of the former contents was now left. Death was walking beside them, step for step.

At last Challenger began to give in, his flanks were pinched and the hollows over his eyes deep sunken; he rubbed his nose against Duncan's arm, whinnied, and looked pleadingly at him. These are the things to break a man's heart in the wilderness. Still there was nothing in sight but the heat-haze and the tall columns of dust raised by the wandering whirlwinds that crossed their track. A false step and the horse went down. McIntyre tried to get him up, but Challenger was too far gone—he must proceed alone. Wetting his lips with a few drops of the water fast evaporating from the bag, he went forward on the course he had been keeping.

Suddenly, right in front of him, rose a small flock of birds. They wheeled and chattered and settled down again! It could only mean water, for since leaving camp he had seen no living thing, and now he recognised the birds as spur-winged plover.

With perspiration nearly blinding him, he staggered on, and then he must have crossed the crest of an almost imperceptible rise, for before him the plain was covered with sheets of shallow water. He had reached the extreme edge of the thunderstorm.

When Duncan lifted his face from the tepid pool after slaking his thirst, his first thought was of the dying horse on the plain. He filled his felt hat and the bag, and dragged himself back to his dumb companion. Challenger lifted his head when he saw him, and whinnied piteously. Four times more he made the journey backwards and forwards, and then the plucky horse managed to get on its legs and follow him down to the water. There was a solitary coolibah tree not far off, and in the miserable shade that it afforded Duncan sat down and tried to eat some of the dried horse-flesh he had brought with him. He was conscious of a fearful headache, for he had been bareheaded when carrying the water to Challenger. He must get back as soon as possible, for the water on the plain was but a few inches deep and fast disappearing. Still he must spell his horse, for after such an ordeal the colt would not carry him half way without rest. At last he felt too stupid to think, and sank into a sleep that lasted until sundown. His head was still throbbing painfully when he awoke, and he arose and bathed it in one of the pools, but the water was warm and afforded him no relief. Challenger seemed greatly recovered, and was feeding on the dry Mitchell grass.

One thought haunted Duncan during the ensuing night of pain—the scorching ride back over the drought-smitten country. Suddenly a whisper seemed to come from the darkness, 'Why go back?' To the eastward the country was well watered, and a few easy stages would take him to the Queensland border and safety. Mitford would wait, and at last give him up, start back on some other course, and probably perish. It was one or other of them. The colt would not carry him more than half way back to camp; then he must walk, and the sun would soon make an end of him. All through the dark hours of semidelirium the voices from the surrounding solitude kept up the refrain, 'Why go back?'

On the fifth day after McIntyre's departure Mitford started on Duncan's tracks with a pack-horse laden with water, hoping to encounter him. The pool was falling rapidly and in a few days would be dry. Fifteen miles from camp he thought he saw a figure moving towards him. It could only be McIntyre, for in that solitude there was no living soul but themselves. He hastily dismounted and, water-bag in hand, hurried to meet him. Duncan did not know him; he was blindly, instinctively following his tracks back to the camp, and it was not until Mitford had poured the water over his head and breast and down his baked throat that his bloodshot eyes lost some of their wildness. His friend had dragged him out of the sun into the only shade there was on that bare plain—beneath the belly of the pack-horse. Here he lay a while with his eyes half closed. At last he began to speak coherently.

'I've got back, old man. Follow my tracks out and you will get to the water, but be quick, for it's drying up fast. Poor old Challenger! I shot him—it was all I could do for him; he never gave in until he was dying.'

His head fell back on his friend's knee, and he was silent for a time. 'I must go on,' he muttered presently. 'Blast that sun! it has done for me; but I will get back'—and he struggled to rise. Mitford kept him down, and he sank into unconsciousness once more.

An hour passed during which Mitford kept pouring water over the burning head; then Duncan opened his eyes and his friend saw that his senses had returned. 'Mitford, old man, I tell you that you must go back to camp and start at once, or it will be late, too late. The water is so shallow it will dry up in a day or two. Poor old Challenger, you'll see his body as you go; but start now and you'll get home safe. That other fellow is going another road. Goodbye.'

THE STOLEN COLOURS

AN exclusively male society, such as ours was on the Baroma River, is apt to get along very smoothly for years, provided that all of the individuals composing it are fairly companionable. There were five stations on the Baroma, all cattle-stations. Sheep had been tried on the country but without success, and now the only marks of their former presence were some roofless huts and the bare patches of ground where once stood sheep-yards; for it was before the days of fences and boundary-riders. Three of the stations were managed by their owners; the other two belonged to Sydney and Melbourne firms, and were in the charge of superintendents, of whom I was one.

Markwell, the other superintendent, was perhaps the only man who did not quite fit in to our little coterie. There was no gainsaying his smartness and ability, but he had a bad temper, and an evil habit of sneering.

Elliot, the owner of Bendalla, the largest station on the river, was a widower. He had one son, who lived on the station with him, and two daughters, who at the time of my story had just arrived on a protracted visit, and created quite an upset in the hitherto even tenor of our way.

Hayward, who owned Pixie, the next station to the one I was managing, was a professed woman-hater, and affected to look on the interest displayed in the newcomers with lofty scorn. Kelly, who had the station on the opposite side of the river, called after that stream, Baroma Plains, fell head over ears in love straight away with Mary Elliot, the elder girl, and having successfully persuaded that young lady that she was in as hopeless a condition, in less than three months their engagement was a proclaimed fact.

Agnes Elliot was two years younger than her engaged sister, and of a very different character. Both were handsome girls, but Mary was easy-going and good-tempered to a fault, while Agnes was of a more active and passionate nature. A tale of wrong that would win from Mary a few compassionate remarks, would wring hot indignation from Agnes.

Jack Elliot, their brother, had always been my especial mate on the river, and naturally on the arrival of his sisters I was thrown a good deal into their society; nor was it long before I learned to love the bright and eager Agnes with a love that could never have been inspired in me by her placid sister. I kept my secret, as I thought, very well, for I had no more prospect of marrying on the extremely limited screw of a cattle-station super. than I had of being made Governor. I might even have got over the fit altogether and cured myself by enforced absence, but for the rivalry of Markwell.

He was my senior by some four or five years had travelled more, and had far more social qualities, when he chose to exert them, than I had; but no better worldly position to recommend him, and knowing the real nature of the man I felt that to suffer him to win such a girl as Agnes Elliot would be a downright wrong to her.

That, you may say, is always the way in which the jealous man argues. Men do not love women so deeply as they hate their rivals in the affections of those women. Marriage is more often the result of a man's determination to avoid injury to his own *amour propre* than of anything else.

Kelly and Mary Elliot were duly married, Baroma Plains rejoiced in a new house and other embellishments, and I was still uncertain as to whether the wayward heart of Agnes inclined to me or not. She had come over to stay with her sister for a while, and one evening I rode across the river ostensibly to see Kelly on some station-business. That was one of the evenings that has ever dwelt in my memory. Never had Agnes been so kind to me. Kelly and his bride, with whom I was first favourite, left us much to ourselves, and half a dozen times an avowal of my love was on my lips. How different things might have been had I spoken then!

She came on to the verandah to say 'Good night!' to me when I left. For a moment I lingered with her warm hand in mine, and her bright eyes looking at me from the dusky shadow of the verandah; then, with sudden desperation, I pressed her hands to my lips and, with a broken 'Good night!' hurried to my horse, mounted, and rode away. She was still standing in the doorway as I turned for a last look, and waved her hand in reply to my salute; and I rode home, the happiest man on the river. When I entered my small sitting-room I saw that, during my absence, the mail had arrived, for the station-bag was lying on the table. I opened it without much interest in the contents, for I was quite absorbed in a dream of Agnes, but was rather surprised to find among the ordinary correspondence a letter from my only brother in England, with whom I had not corresponded for years—not from any quarrel, but simply through the disinclination to write that grows on most men in the bush. The letter had been delayed through going to a former address. The contents were important, as they notified to me the death of an uncle, who had left his money to my brother and myself and two cousins.

My first thought naturally was that now I was in a position to propose to Agnes, and I lay awake all night, determined that not many hours of daylight should elapse ere I was over at Baroma Plains.

The next morning the delays seemed never-ending. Horses had escaped from the paddock, a blackboy got bucked off and broke his collar-bone, which I had to set, and a messenger came over from Hayward with a letter requiring a reply. It was eleven o'clock ere I was once more in sight of the verandah where I had last seen Agnes.

Mrs. Kelly met me with her usual kind smile. Agnes had gone home nearly an hour ago. Jack Elliot had come up for her in a hurry, as his father was starting down to port and wanted Agnes to go down with him. I hesitated whether to go on to Bendalla on the chance of overtaking them, but my presence was absolutely necessary on the station: I could not leave without going back first.

'When will they be back?' I asked, blushing, as I thought that my fair hostess was doubtless reading me like a book.

'They will stop until the races. You know we are all going down, and you must come with us.'

The local races were coming off in about a week at the little shipping port; and most of us on the river had entered horses for the occasion. I thanked Mrs. Kelly for her invitation, which I gladly accepted, and, without telling my news, rode home.

Only a week! but it loomed before me like a year. I could not even write, for we had only a weekly mail, and I would be down myself by that time. To add to my annoyance, Markwell, whose place was at the head of the river, came over that night, on his way down to port. I managed to be civil to him, but when I saw him ride away in the morning to the township, where he would be within call of Agnes for the whole week during which I should be tied to the station, I felt inclined to try on him the range of my new rifle. Hayward came to see me next day, and to him I confided the news of my inheritance. He had been talking of going out west and taking up some country for which, at that time, there was a great rush, and he urged me to accompany him now that I had the means. He was a shrewd man, for whom I had a great liking, and I promised to weigh the matter carefully.

At last the time came when I could fling dull care aside, and, seated on the box beside Kelly, relieving him occasionally of the task of tooling four horses along an abominable road, I felt that every mile brought me nearer to the consummation of my hopes. Arrived in the little port which in those days had not assumed its present dimensions or importance, my first thought, after I had made myself presentable, was naturally to call upon Mr. Elliot. The family, including Kelly and his wife, were located in the house of a friend, a widower, with one little girl, whose habitation was far too big for him. Agnes was out—gone out for a ride with her brother and Markwell.

This was a check at the start.

While chatting with Elliot the party returned, and, with a very sore feeling in my heart, the meeting I had been so longing for came off.

How bright and handsome she looked in her close-fitting riding-habit as she came along the verandah and greeted me! Every jealous thought in my mind would have been exorcised but for the presence of Markwell, who gave me a supercilious nod and looked on with an air of insolent proprietorship—at least I thought so—while the ordinary commonplace words were exchanged. She noticed instinctively the change in my manner and her pride took fire. Ah! these wretched conceits of self, which do work we can never undo!

I stayed to dinner with the Elliots, but had no opportunity to speak to Agnes until some time afterwards, when by chance I saw her sitting apart from the others in the drawing-room with the little girl, the daughter of their host, at her knee. She was stitching industriously at some ribbon and I lost not a minute in reaching her side.

'What is the work, Miss Elliot?' I said rather awkwardly to break the ice.

'My colours for to-morrow's races,' she returned.

'And who is to wear them?' I asked, bending down and speaking earnestly.

'That depends,' she answered, glancing up at me with a smile that put every sore feeling to flight, for I knew they were meant for me.

'So we have to congratulate you, Murray,' said the hateful voice of Markwell close behind.

I turned sharply round, and Agnes flushed quickly, for his words seemed to have a double meaning.

'What do you mean?' I asked, rather rudely.

'Why, they say you have come in to a pot of money. Is it true?'

So some gabbling idiot from the station had brought the yarn down and now it was blurted out like this when I had meant to tell Agnes just when I asked her to be my wife! I replied very shortly that an uncle of mine was dead from whom I inherited some money; but my chance was spoilt, and if it had been my rival's object to break up our chat, he succeeded admirably. I guessed that Agnes was hurt that I had not told her brother or father, who had so long been my friends, of my good fortune, not divining my reason for keeping silence.

Next morning the whole township was on the race course. I rode out the two miles with Jack Elliot, for Kelly had his trap full. I wondered whether Agnes had entrusted the knot of ribbons to her brother, but apparently he was charged with no such mission; so I took the earliest opportunity of presenting myself before the party as soon as I saw them arrive I had promised to steer a horse of Kelly's in the hurdle race, for, as a newly married man, all such pleasures had been sternly denied him, and Markwell, who was a sporting man, had entered a horse of his own.

It was in vain that I lingered around the buggy. Agnes several times seemed on the point of speaking to me confidentially, but something always interfered, and I had at last to go away unsatisfied as the time for our race was approaching.

I had donned my jacket, or rather Kelly's, when the man himself came into the tent.

'Now, then, Davie,' he said, 'just one word. I want to win this race, and you can do it if you race Markwell right away from the jump. The others have no show; his horse has more foot than Beeswax (Kelly's horse), but he can't fly his jumps like old Bee can, and if you make it hot from the start, he'll either come to grief or drive you home.'

I signified my comprehension, and was leaving the tent when he added: 'By the way, Mary gave me a message for you from Agnes—something about having lost something; however, she can tell you herself after you've won the race;' and so we sallied forth, I much puzzled at the meaning of the half-forgotten message.

Markwell was already mounted and had taken his horse over a hurdle, and was walking him back when I passed him, and there, on the breast of his jacket, was the identical knot of black-and-orange ribbons I had seen Agnes putting together the night before.

The sight roused every jealous passion within me; I knew they must be the same, or else why had I not received them according to the half promise made?

'I'll win this race or break Markwell's neck,' I muttered to Kelly as he gave me a leg into the saddle. He squeezed my hand, and the next moment Beeswax was over the hurdle like a swallow.

There were six of us in the race, but Markwell's horse was the only one I dreaded. We had a good start although Beeswax, excited by his canter, was dancing to get off. I took the lead at once at a pace that few hurdle races are ever ridden, and for half a mile kept it, without seeing a horse, Beeswax taking his jumps just as a matter of course. At the end of the half-mile I heard a rap and a clatter, and glancing round found Markwell just behind me.

His horse had twice the pace of Beeswax and he had bustled him over the jumps so far without coming to grief. On the flat he raced up to me without an effort and I knew that my only chance was to rush him at the hurdles. Twice his horse blundered dreadfully, and I was well ahead when we were two jumps from home. If he got over those two jumps safely I was beaten, for he would catch me on the straight run in.

I knew Markwell's horse was as excitable as he could be, so I pulled Beeswax a little and let him come up and get about half a length ahead, then I put Beeswax at the next jump 'all I knew,' and he seemed to take the hurdle in his stride. Not so my rival's mount; maddened with the rush of the other horse alongside of him, he scarcely attempted to jump and went down headlong, but fortunately for his rider, sending him rolling ahead.

The others were all out of it, so I pulled Beeswax in; put him quietly over the last hurdle and cantered past the winning-post.

'He's all right,' said Kelly, as he came and took my bridle to lead me in to be weighed, 'but he got a devil of a purler.'

Strange to say, Markwell had escaped almost without a bruise. He had been flung forward, a little to one side, just as the horse was in the act of turning over, and had rolled out of harm's way. The saddle was smashed, and the horse could never be got to face a jump again, but I was really glad that no worse accident had happened.

He came up pluckily, in spite of his shaking, and forced a jesting remark about the pace we had ridden. I changed my jacket, and after the usual noisy congratulations, found my way up to Mrs. Kelly and Agnes.

'Your colours were unlucky, Miss Elliot,' I said, regretting the words the next moment.

'My colours, Mr. Murray! I did not know they were in the race.'

'Mr. Markwell wore them, at any rate,' I answered, rather surprised.

'You are joking,' she replied; 'and I don't think it in good taste.'

I drew back, snubbed and offended. Mrs. Kelly put her hand on my shoulder as I stood beside the buggy, and, stooping down, whispered to me, quite energetically for her,

'Davie, don't be a fool.'

I guessed her meaning, and if I could have made my peace then, I would; but I was not afforded the opportunity. Agnes kept me at a distance for the rest of the day.

There was a race-ball that night, and I fondly hoped that I should have a chance of an explanation. Markwell, in spite of the heavy fall he had experienced, was there, and exerting all the agreeable qualities he possessed to the utmost.

Agnes gave me no excuse for trying to get a moment's private conversation, and in the course of the evening I was lounging in a sulky fit on the verandah, when I saw her and Markwell in deep conversation in a secluded part of it. She was speaking earnestly, although I could not see the expression of her face. I had seen enough, however, for my then temper; apparently she had afforded him the benefit of the confidential interview that she had avoided giving me. I left the ball, and a month afterwards Hayward and I were out west. I stayed out there two years. I heard from Kelly and Jack Elliot, but the name of Agnes seemed carefully tabooed in their letters.

One evening I received a visit from an old friend who had a station not very far from the little port where my love-dream had been shattered. He had taken up country beyond Hayward and me, and was on his road to port when he called.

'By the way,' he said, 'you may remember Markwell who got such a spill at the races that time; but, of course, you do, as you rode against him.'

I nodded assent, and he went on.

'I heard he had come out this way to take up country for his firm.'

'He didn't marry Miss Elliot then?' I said in as easy a voice as I could command.

'I should think not,' replied my friend, 'she found him out in a most shabby trick. I'll tell you all about it. You remember the ball after the races? I was out on the verandah behind a screen of plants and flags doing a quiet flirtation, when Miss Elliot and Markwell came on the other side. We couldn't well get out and had to sit there and listen to what they were saying. It seems he had bribed the little girl at the house where the Elliots were staying to steal a knot of ribbon that Miss Elliot had made for somebody else and he had worn it openly at the races as though she had given it to him. That young lady could be very indignant when she liked, and I shouldn't have liked the sarcasm she lashed Markwell with.'

I was silent for some time, while Russel smoked vigorously, recalling the scene.

'I'm tired of this place,' I suddenly said; 'I'll go down to port with you.'

'That's famous,' he returned, 'I wanted a mate down.' And he turned in while I commenced my preparations.

Half-way across what was known as 'the dry stage' was a shanty, professedly an accommodation house; but, of course, a slygrog shop. The man who kept it met us outside the rude thatched verandah and said he was glad we had come, as there was a man inside who had 'a touch of the sun' and he was afraid he was going to die.

We went in to see the poor fellow, and there, on the frowsy bunk, lay my old rival, Markwell. The man said he arrived the day before, on foot; his horse had fallen with him and got away, and he had walked on to borrow another to go after him. He was light-headed and had been so ever since.

Russel and I sat up all night doing what we could, but it was useless; the poor fellow died before morning. Once he recognised me and laughed wildly, 'You didn't get Agnes after all, Murray,' he said, then he relapsed into mad talk about racing.

*   *   *

It was a lovely evening when, with my heart in my mouth, I rode up to Baroma Plains, for I preferred to see Mrs. Kelly first. She and her husband were standing on the verandah watching me curiously as I came up. Suddenly Kelly gave a wild whoop and sprang off the verandah. 'It's Davie, by gum!' he exclaimed, and I was soon standing between them.

I looked hard at Mrs. Kelly, hoping she would take pity on me, but I had to ask the question after all.

'Agnes?'

Kelly pursed up his lips, 'Don't you know?' he asked.

'Know what?' I demanded, swallowing a big lump in my throat.

'Why, Agnes was married a year ago—she lives—let's see—in Melbourne!'

I suppose I could not smile, nor even look cheerful, for kind Mrs. Kelly broke in with, 'It's a shame. Nothing of the sort, Davie. Agnes Elliot is in there just now; and to tell you the truth, she must have recognised you before we did, for she slipped in without a word when you were a long way off. Go in and ask her.'

I did not ask her. I only said one word, and that was her Christian name; and when I took her in my arms for the first time we forgot all about mutual explanation until some time afterwards.

BUNTHORP'S DECEASE

I.

'WRITES poetry, does he?'

'Yes, and worse.'

'Worse? Impossible!'

'Tries to set it to music, and accompanies himself on the concertina.'

'Great heavens! I must see about it. Deane was a real good fellow, and I can't let his son go to the dogs without an attempt to save him. Tell Billy to run up Rocket and Revolver from the big paddock first thing in the morning.'

So spoke old Bunthorp, of Wattlemere Station, as he and his nephew yarned on the verandah one evening, after the return of the latter from attending a general muster at Branksia Downs, some forty miles distant.

Bunthorp shortly retired to bed, and Jim Newton strolled over to 'the quarters,' to play euchre for tobacco, any higher stakes being strictly forbidden on Wattlemere.

Next morning saw the old man seated in a buck-board buggy behind Rocket and Revolver, trotting sedately along the road, winding through alternate belts of scrub and plain, that separated the two stations.

'Awful thing,' he thought, as he sipped the midday quart of tea at 'the yellow water hole,' rather more than half-way. 'Fancy Deane's boy taking to scribbling poetry. Why, the cattle will go to the deuce in no time. I don't believe Deane ever wrote anything but a horse-receipt or his name to a cheque.'

Musing thus on his dead friend the old gentleman dropped off into a pleasant doze under a sheltering brigalow tree, while Rocket and Revolver, carefully hobbled out, stood nose to tail in an adjacent patch of scrub, sleepily whisking the flies off each other.

'I say, guv'nor!'

Old Bunthorp opened his eyes and looked sternly at the disturber of his forty winks. A swagman with 'genus sundowner' written all over him, had cast his rolled blanket on the ground and was busy putting together the smouldering sticks that had boiled Bunthorp's quart-pot.

'S'pose you'll give a fellow a feed?' he remarked.

Bunthorp nodded majestically, as if to impress the man with the idea that he had only closed his eyes for a few minutes in order to meditate better over the advantage of only a first cross of Herefords; but the new-comer, quite unimpressed, strolled down to the water to fill the small 'billy' he was carrying. When he returned, Bunthorp was just starting off with the winkers in his hand to catch his horses; he indicated the remainder of the bread and beef to the man, who acknowledged the favour with an easy nod as he piled the blazing sticks around his billy to facilitate a speedy boil. When the old gentleman returned with the nags the stranger enquired for the tea and sugar with the cool familiarity of an acquaintance. 'Not a bad sort of a prad that brown one,' he remarked; 'looks a little gone in the near fore-leg.'

Bunthorp was speechless. Rocket, the prad in question, was rising five and as sound as a bell. He slipped on the collars whilst the swagman made and sweetened his tea. Then he busied himself putting the contents of the buggy straight. Meantime his uninvited guest attacked the bread and beef.

'How far to Branksia Downs?' he said, as Bunthorp was preparing to start.

'About fifteen miles.'

'You wouldn't give a fellow a lift, would you? I'm dog-tired.'

Now, Bunthorp was the best-natured of men, and, moreover, was never slow in boasting how he had risen from the ranks himself; but the idea of driving up to Banksia Downs homestead with this disreputable-looking dead-beat beside him, was rather a staggerer. He hesitated.

'Come, guv'nor, if you knew how just about done up I am, you wouldn't think twice. What's my weight to two such bits of stuff as those?'

'Well, look sharp and finish your grub,' said the old fellow, 'I won't wait long.'

The seedy stranger made but a few bites of the remainder, swallowed his tea scalding hot, without winking, and in a few minutes took his seat with the greatest coolness beside James Bunthorp, Esq., of Wattlemere.

Rocket and Revolver soon covered the fifteen miles, the swagman beguiling the way with a little general advice on pastoral matters, hints as to breeding, &c., winding up by urging his disgusted companion to always drive with a cross-bar on the pole in future. In fact, when they arrived at the paddock-gate, half a mile from the station, Bunthorp could scarcely determine whether he had given the stranger a lift, or the stranger had given him one. At the gate he saw his opportunity. The man got down to open it. 'I will send your swag to the men's hut,' said Bunthorp, as whipping up his horses he drove on, leaving the discomfited wayfarer to close the gate and follow on foot.

'Well, Fred, my boy,' said the old man, as a young fellow came out to greet him. 'Heard such terrible accounts of you from Jim that I had to come over myself and see about it.'

'What has Jim been saying?' returned the other, as he shook him heartily by the hand. 'But come inside first; George will see to the buggy and horses. Glory! what sort of a swag is that you've got on board?'

'Oh! I gave a fellow a lift on the road There he is, coming up the paddock now. Give him his swag, George, when he comes up,' he continued to the groom, and then both men went inside the house.

'Have you got any of the old whisky left, Fred, or was it all swamped this muster?'

'Not quite!' returned the other; 'rather too good for the general public, who only want something that bites as it goes down. No fear, here we are.'

'His heart is in the right place,' murmured old Bunthorp as he put the amber-coloured fluid to his lips. 'Your father and I bought this whisky in bond six years ago,' he continued aloud. 'Unfortunately my share is gone, but—here's to his memory. Now, Fred, I must speak seriously.'

'Suppose we wait until after dinner, it will be ready at six. I just want to run down to the yard for a minute; meantime you know your old room. Go and rinse some of the dust off.'

'Seems nothing wrong with him—wonder if Jim has been taking a rise out of me!' thought the old man, as he turned into the bedroom he generally occupied. 'My word!'

There had been some changes in the interior arrangements of Branksia since his last visit, and young Deane had forgotten that he had transferred his own belongings to the former guest-chamber; consequently, when Bunthorp turned into what he thought was his room, he found himself in Fred's. But this had not occasioned the exclamation. Fred's room in its simple bareness was quite familiar to him. There was the collection of whips, the rows of boots, from a dandified pair of tops that he once rode a steeplechase in, to the reach-me-down bluchers that he wore in the drafting-yard, a few native weapons, a picture of Carbine, and the necessary furniture—that was all as it should be. But there was something fresh—a new picture on the wall: a photograph got up and finished in the style these things are done now-a-days—the likeness of an exceedingly pretty girl.

Bunthorp picked up his valise again and beat a retreat, chuckling. 'The young dog, won't I roast him!' And it was only after three or four immersions in cold water that he managed to wash the sly look out of his jolly face.

Meantime Deane was astonished to find no one at the yard. There were a few head of cattle to be drafted, some outsiders, missed during the muster, and he wished to draft them overnight, so that the calves could be branded at daylight in the morning. A sustained yell brought two or three men out of the hut.

'Nearly forgot all about the cattle, Mr. Deane,' said one, as he swung himself over the cap. 'Blessed if we were not all laughing so at that cure of a fellow Mr. Bunthorp gave a lift to.'

'Regular bush lawyer,' said another.

'Then he won't get a job from me,' replied Deane, as he picked up the draftingpole and opened the gate.

'Job!' said the man who had first spoken, 'he don't want no job—lives upon blow.'

At dinner Bunthorp was brimming over with facetiousness. Mysterious allusions to a coming volume of poetry, to the expense of re-furnishing the house and building 'a weaning paddock' (nursery), to breaking in side-saddle horses, and various other old jokes, at which he laughed so much himself that Fred had to join him.

'Now, when is it to be!' he said when they were seated in the verandah doing the regulation-pipe.

Fred felt glad it was comparatively dark, for the old man's fun was rather merciless.

'I suppose,' he said, 'that beggar Jim has been telling tales about me.'

'He said you had taken to writing poetry, to spouting it, and singing it to a concertina.'

'Confounded old ass he must be! I only asked him his opinion on a few lines of verse, and as for the concertina business—why, we were just trying to pick out a tune together. But I suppose I may as well own up—I am engaged.'

'Who is she, Fred?'

'Come in to the light,' returned Deane; and going to his room he returned with the portrait Bunthorp had seen hanging on the wall. 'Do you know her?' he asked, as Bunthorp regarded it admiringly and curiously.

'I seem to recognise the face,' said the old gentleman; 'seems as familiar as possible now and again, and then it's all different.'

'You have not seen her for five years, and she was only thirteen then—.'

'Not Maggie Barlow?' cried Bunthorp, with the fun gone clean out of his face and voice.

'Certainly it is. Why, she used to be your greatest pet at one time.'

'Ah, that was before Deane found Barlow out. I admit I did like her immensely, as a child; but you can't alter a bad breed, no matter how good-looking the calf is: it will come out by-and-bye.'

Fred coloured, although he also felt inclined to laugh. 'Of course, I stand you saying things I would not let anybody else utter; but you're very unjust, to say the least of it.'

'Unjust! Why? Was I not acquainted with the whole of the circumstances? Did not your father confide everything to me, and, by my advice, did not prosecute him? Only for me, Fred Barlow would now be in prison. Your father was not a merciful man, you know, although nobody could be juster.'

'I know the man yielded to a great temptation, and he has bitterly repented it ever since,' returned Deane; 'but I believe, and I think you do, that it was done to save his son.'

'That's another pretty thing,' cried the old gentleman, who was now excitedly walking up and down the room. 'You mark my words: so soon as ever you are married, that precious scamp will turn up and sponge on you.'

'I think you know me better than that. Am I such a weak-minded individual?'

'No, Fred, you've got plenty of backbone; but he'll try it on. He'll hear of it, even if he's in Pentridge or Darlinghurst.'

'I think he must be dead. Maggie has not heard his name mentioned for years. But we won't talk any more to-night. Sleep on it, and I know you'll give me your best wishes in the morning.'

Half-an-hour afterwards Deane was alone, strolling about in front of the verandah, smoking and thinking of the late conversation. The night was dead calm, and the voices from the men's quarters sounded clear and distinct; one in particular, which he could not recognise, seemed to monopolise the conversation.

'The bush lawyer, I suppose,' thought Fred, and by way of amusement he sauntered within hearing. The men were lounging about in the broad verandah of the kitchen, and the traveller was holding forth.

'Bunthorp! Who's Bunthorp?' he was saying; 'why, you coves seem to think that he's the Hemperor of China. Now, I'll bet you a fiver all round'—here there was a burst of laughter—'What are you laughing at?' demanded the unabashed swagman.

'Produce your fivers, old man,' said one of his audience.

'Well, I ain't got 'em about me just now,' returned the shabby stranger, 'but I would bet you if I had 'em that you give old Bunthorp a French book to read and he won't understand a word of it, and give it to me and I'll translate it straight off the reel. Yet he drives his buggy and I have to walk.'

'Except when he gives you a lift,' said the cook.

'Hang his lift!' returned the other. 'Mighty generous thing to do with a couple of fat, strong horses in the traces.'

'I don't know whether he understands French or not,' said the stockman, 'and I don't care, but he's a decent old boy, and I wish there were a few more of his sort knocking about the district.'

'Decent old boy!' sneered the swagman. 'Who couldn't be decent with a good-paying station and a fat balance in the bank?'

'Plenty of 'em,' said the cook. 'I know lots far richer than Bunthorp who are as mean as you make 'em.'

'Just so,' returned the traveller, 'and the worst of it is, it's catching. Now, if old Bunthorp came to you and said "Bill, I'm short of change; lend me a note," you'd say, "certainly, Mr. Bunthorp, take two," now, wouldn't you?'

'Of course I would, if I had it.'

'Of course you would, and if I came to you and said "Bill, I'm stone broke; lend me a note till I get a job," what would you say?'

There was an ominous silence; then the stockman reared up his long, lean form, and, knocking the ashes out of his pipe, remarked; 'I'm going to camp; we've got to be up the first thing to brand those calves, boys.'

There was a general dispersal, and the disgusted swagman was left with his question unanswered.

'I wonder,' thought Deane, as he made his way to bed, 'how it is that that fellow's voice is so familiar to me? Bad egg, I suppose, who speaks like a gentleman by accident now and again.'

II.

Barlow had been Crown Lands Commissioner in the neighbouring township five years before. He was a widower, with one girl, but people who knew anything said that the Barlow who got three years for embezzlement from one of the banks was his son. It was a much-talked-of case, from the despicable efforts made by the culprit, who was bank-teller, to put the guilt on to an innocent man. Deane and Bunthorpe knew the truth, for they had been fast friends of the commissioner until the fatal day when a broken, miserable man rode to Branksia Downs and confessed to the owner that he had used his name criminally to obtain money; and gave him back the price of his shame. Bunthorp, who was there, believed that it was a mad attempt, made too late, to save his son from disgrace, and begged his old friend, whose nature was less placable, to take the money and spare the unfortunate father. Deane did so, Barlow applied for a change, and his name was never willingly mentioned by the two who had been his friends. All these things came into Bunthorp's mind before he fell asleep; and as the old man knew, too, that black sheep were to be found in nearly every flock, he gradually came round to the opinion that possibly a young fellow like Deane, with his head screwed on right, could not come to much grief by marrying a girl like Maggie, whose only fault was a disgraced brother, and a father prematurely broken down by that son's disgrace. Before Bunthorp fell asleep, he had in spirit bestowed a fatherly blessing on the young people.

Fate seemed determined that his slumbers should not be as calm as his conscience merited. Somebody touched him, somebody whispered, 'Mr. Deane!'

Bunthorp was not nervous, he had gone through too many rough episodes. 'Who is there?' he asked in an equally low tone.

'Bell! Sergeant Bell! We are after somebody, and I think he's here. I don't want to disturb the place or he might give us the slip. Any strangers here to-night?'

'I'm Bunthorp. Fred has changed his room. There was a traveller on the road. I gave him a lift. He's here to-night, I suppose.'

'Where did you pick him up?' said the sergeant, still in a whisper.

'At the yellow water-hole.'

'Yes, that's where we lost his tracks; we guessed you might have picked him up, so we came straight on here. I suppose he's in the men's hut. But I'm glad I saw you first'—this was allegorical, for it was pitch-dark—'can you come outside for a minute?' Bunthorp noiselessly slipped on some clothes and, barefooted, followed the policeman, who had also left his boots outside. Out of hearing of the house they put on their foot-gear and went a short distance to where a black tracker stood holding three horses.

'I should like to get this fellow away quietly without troubling Mr. Deane,' said the sergeant, 'now that I have the chance; for I'll tell you who he is: that son of old Barlow's who served his time for the bank swindle.'

Bunthorp whistled. 'What has he been up to?'

'Valueless cheques, for one thing; and doctoring a cheque, for another— turned seven into seventy; very neatly too, I understand. He got a warning from somebody and gave the Brisbane police the slip; he's splendidly got up as a hard-up loafer, and has got all the patter off like a professional hand. No one suspected him but a girl at the Royal, in ——, who knew him in his bank days. She gave him away. Of course, you know, Deane is sweet on the sister, so I should like to take him quietly for both their sakes.'

'Very thoughtful of you, Bell, I am sure;' said Bunthorp; 'how can we manage it?'

'We can't take him now without waking the place, and if we wait till daylight he might give us the slip—he's so artful,' returned Bell.

'Deane will be down at the yard for an hour or two after daylight, there are a few calves to brand. Could you manage it then?'

'I think so, it's not more than two hours off daylight now. We'll turn our horses out behind that patch of scrub, and be up there at crow-chirp and catch my gentleman in his blankets as soon as the others go down to the yard. There's an old hut alongside the kitchen we can plant in.'

'I'll slip in and get you a bit of grub, our supper is still on the table,' said the hospitable Mr. Bunthorp, and like a substantial phantom he disappeared in the darkness, and presently returned with some provender and a drop of the incomparable whisky, which he had smuggled out without wakening Deane, the only other occupant of the house. Bunthorp had no desire to return to bed, but shared the sergeant's watch until the first streak of light in the eastern horizon warned them to be on the alert. Quietly they stationed themselves in the old hut, whence, through the chinks between the slabs, they could see what went on.

It was done without any trouble at all. Deane and his men were busy at the yard, when Bell stood over the sleeper and requested the pleasure of his company. Before they started, Bunthorp got leave to say a few words privately to the prisoner.

'I know who you are,' he said, 'and for your father's sake, whom you nearly ruined, I should like to do something for you. What can I do? I presume you are guilty of this charge?'

Barlow looked at him with his manner partly changed; and the old man noted with sorrow the likeness to his sister, which he now saw plainly. 'I may get out of this,' was the answer, 'I think there's a legal quibble or two in my favour; if I do, may I ask a favour of you?'

'Yes, I will do what I can. What is it?'

'When the time comes I will ask it,' and he turned away. Next minute the sergeant and his prisoner were gone.

When Fred came up to breakfast, he was in blissful ignorance that his prospective brother-in-law had just been marched off in handcuffs; and there was some laughter amongst the men when they were told of the swagman's exit.

Bunthorp naturally scanned the papers with some degree of interest, until he saw that Barlow's favourable anticipation had been only partially fulfilled. He had managed to wriggle out of the graver charge, and escaped with twelve months' imprisonment and a severe lecture from the judge for one of the minor offences.

Fred Deane was married, and Bunthorp had beamed on the union. Eighteen months had flown by, when he received a letter he had been for some time expecting; it was from young Barlow, asking for the promised help. The letter touched the good old man. There was no hypocritical pretence of reformation: the writer simply stated his desire to leave Australia and begin life anew in another country, mentioning the Cape as the colony to be honoured with his patronage, and asking for a sum of money to enable him to go there. Needless to say it was at once forwarded; and Bunthorp trusted that that page was folded down for good.

'My dear Fred,' he wrote, some six months afterwards, 'I have just remembered that the 5th of next month is your wife's birthday, so I am coming over the day before to stop the night, and bring a present to deliver the next morning. Don't show this to Maggie, or she may be curious.'

On the evening of the 4th, according to promise, Bunthorp and Jim Newton drove up to Branksia, but the most inquisitive glances cast into the buggy, still drawn by the faithful Rocket and Revolver, could not discern anything unusual in its contents. This was not to be wondered at, for 'the present' was but a letter with a Cape of Good Hope stamp on it, telling of young Barlow's bright prospects, and conveying a kind message to his sister, and an assurance that the future would atone for the past. The old man had a small gift as well, but this was the surprise he had planned. That night he slept in the room made memorable by the visit of Sergeant Bell, and it was with a decidedly nervous start that he found his slumbers once more disturbed. Somebody was moving about the room, apparently examining the contents of the dressing-table. Bunthorp sprang out of bed as fast as a stout, old gentleman, who had been sleeping on his back, could be expected to spring. As this was not very rapidly, the intruder had gone before Bunthorp had reached the spot where his shadowy form had been visible. Bunthorp went out to the verandah, but an outcry of dogs by the stables told him that the pursuit was vain; the quarry had too good a start. Returning to his room he struck a match, and, having lit a candle, proceeded to investigate. Apparently nothing had been taken, but on the table was a leaf from a pocket-book, folded and addressed to himself. 'If you want to save your friend Deane some trouble and distress,' it ran, 'take a walk down the paddock, as far as the gate, before breakfast, as soon after sunrise as possible.'

'Is this Queensland or one of the disturbed districts of Ireland?' muttered the old man savagely, as he got into bed again. 'I'll take a walk down the paddock with a good whip in my hand, and all the dogs with me;' and in a few minutes he was sound asleep again. Like all bushmen he instinctively awoke at daybreak, and, dressing himself, went out just as the red sun appeared above the low tree line. He had a heavy crop in his hand, and a whistle brought at least half-a-dozen demonstrative dogs of all breeds to his heels, eager for a morning gambol.

The paddock-gate was out of sight of the homestead, being screened by some clumps of scrub; leaning against it was a man, who, when he turned and faced the new-comer, revealed to Bunthorp's intense amazement the features of the former swagman, young Barlow.

He was fairly well-dressed, and a good horse was fastened to the fence a few panels away.

'So you've come back from the Cape?' was Bunthorp's exclamation.

'I've never been to the Cape, you old fool!' was the amazing reply. 'That letter was posted by a friend of mine who went there. No; I have got a long score to settle with you before we have done with each other.'

'You d——d thief, you took my money ——' began Bunthorp, violently.

'Yes,' interrupted the other, 'I took your money under false pretences; and I put it on the Melbourne Cup, and, by George, I won, and I intend to get some more out of you, so there.'

'No, I'll be boiled down if you will,' said the old man. 'What score have you to settle with me?'

'Didn't you put that —— sergeant on to me? He told me all about it. When you found out who I was, why didn't you give me warning and get me away? You could easily have managed it. Hang you all your friendship for my father. Between you all I've been shamefully treated, and I intend to take it out of you.'

During this harangue Bunthorp had been, so to say, stoking; he was now at boiling heat and ripe for an explosion. 'You hangdog gaol-bird!' he commenced, 'you been shamefully treated? why, you have never had your desserts yet! Take it out of me, you abominable scoundrel? Why don't you do it?' and he fairly danced with rage.

'Keep cool, old boy,' said Barlow, 'you'll want all your breath before you've done with me. To-day is Maggie's birthday, and I am going to present myself to wish her many happy returns. I can assure you some of my prison anecdotes will quite liven up the conversation, and I really won't stop away under a high consideration.'

'You'll not get a red cent, that I guarantee. Fred Deane is not such a fool as to be blackmailed by you; try it, and see what you'll get,' returned Bunthorp, whose business faculties at once came to the front.

'Oh, but that is not all: you and Fred's father compounded a felony; you know you did. That will be a nice little story to rake up.'

'Whether we broke the law or not I do not know, but every honest man will be on our side, and I don't care a snap of the fingers for the rest.'

The two men looked at each other defiantly across the gate, but the swindler had failed and he knew it. He turned away jauntily. 'Well,' he said airily, 'I'll call round after breakfast, see you again. So long, old Bun.'

This was the crowning insult. Flinging open the gate Bunthorp with upraised whip rushed at the sneering Barlow, while the joyous dogs surged tumultuously around. The two men struggled together and the dogs, wild with delight, sent up a chorus of yelling, barking, and snapping that raised some laggard cur at the station and attracted everybody's attention. Barlow's horse, startled at the uproar, broke his bridle with an indignant snort and trotted away in the bush.

'The dogs have got a kangaroo stuck up at the back of the scrub,' said one of the men, and two or three of them came running down.

Bunthorp had got in several stinging cuts before Barlow seized the whip, and then they struggled hard for the possession of it, the dogs making indiscriminate and quite impartial snaps at the legs of both. The younger man succeeded in wresting the crop from his opponent, who was soon winded; he threw him off and gave him a blow with the butt as he did so, unfortunately on the head. Bunthorp went down senseless and Barlow started to pursue his horse, but the pack of dogs had to be first scattered with the whip. By this time two active men who had taken a short cut through the scrub appeared on the scene. They vaulted over the fence, and as Barlow's horse was now nearly out of sight, he saw it was useless to run, so stood still to await them.

'The old fellow turned on me with his whip, and in the struggle I knocked him down,' he said, when they reached the spot. They bent over Bunthorp, and one of them gave a loud coo-ee that brought others down—amongst them Deane and Newton. They carried the old man up to the house and marched Barlow along. He did not reveal himself, although some of them recognised him with surprise as the swagman.

Once at the station he requested to see Deane alone, and told him who he was, asserting that it was only in self-defence he had struck Bunthorp, which was literally true, and insisting on being allowed to depart in search of his horse. Deane was rather puzzled; he compromised matters by sending a blackboy after the horse and telling his brother-in-law that he would not allow him to leave until Bunthorp was conscious: meantime, if he wanted any assistance, he had better keep himself quiet and not attempt to see his sister.

Between them, Mrs. Deane and Newton had now recalled the unconscious Bunthorp to life once more. 'I gave it to him, Jim,' were the first words he spoke. 'Called me old Bun.' Then he lay back and closed his eyes. Presently he opened them again; 'Maggie,' he said, 'I want to be alone with Jim for a minute.' Mrs. Deane nodded and left the room. 'Look here, Jim,' said the old man eagerly: 'I'm going to die.'

'Go to blazes!' replied his astonished nephew.

'In about an hour's time I shall expire,' repeated his uncle. 'No, I'm not wandering. I'm in solemn earnest. Do you think you could get me a drop of that old whisky; I feel faint?'

Newton, with astonishment all over his face, left the room, and Bunthorp went off into a series of chuckles; evidently he had got hold of a brilliant idea.

His nephew returned, and Bunthorp swallowed the spirits. 'What's become of that fellow?' he asked.

'Deane has locked him up somewhere.'

'Right! Now, Jim, I'll explain myself. So far as dying is concerned, it would take more than a knock like that to kill me; but that scamp is young Barlow, who, of course, you've heard of. Now, he can't do any real harm, and Fred is not the man to be sponged on and robbed, but he might make things unpleasant. People would talk, Maggie would feel it, and there might be trouble between husband and wife, because, after all, people are only human. Now, if I die—you twig? Barlow will stand his trial for murder. Deane gives him a chance to clear out and he'll take care never to show up in Queensland again, where he'll think there's a halter waiting for him. Savee, James?' And the restored Bunthorp dug his amazed nephew in the ribs.

Barlow was confined in the store; he had been reposing on the top of a pile of flourbags reading a yellow-back, for some time, when the door opened and Deane appeared. He appeared greatly excited. 'The old man is dead,' he said hurriedly, 'I can't see you hanged, for you're Maggie's brother after all. Your horse is tied up at the paddock gate, the men are at dinner, slip down through the scrub and be off before Newton comes, for he's going to take you into the police-camp himself.'

'But,' said the other, 'it was only manslaughter; he attacked me. I'll stand my trial.'

'You infernal fool, what show have you got? Look at your character, who saw him strike you? who will believe you? The men took you red-handed with the whip in your hand. Stay and be hanged if you like. Newton will swear your life away, he's furious.'

'I have very little money,' said Barlow sullenly.

'Here, take this; it is enough to pay your passage, and give you a start somewhere. Now, for God's sake go, before it is too late.'

Barlow moved to the door; he was beginning to grasp the situation, and didn't like it.

'Keep off the roads,' said Deane, 'and slip out of the country like greased lightning; everybody liked Bunthorp and they will search high and low for you.'

Deane stood at the door as though keeping watch; he saw his brother-in-law disappear in the first patch of scrub, and that was the last he ever saw of him.

Few livelier corpses have ever been seen at a dinner-table than Bunthorp's was that evening. Newton said that 'a crack on the cobra' must have a more stimulating effect on the brain than any amount of the incomparable whisky.

THE STORY OF A BIG PEARL

LAZILY riding at anchor, in company with some half-dozen others, is a small lugger, one of a pearling fleet. It is almost a dead calm, and on the northern horizon there is a hazy suspicion of land, the coast of New Guinea. The midday spell is drawing to a close, and the coloured crew are rousing themselves from their short nap under the awning stretched amidships. In the cabin, permeated, as is all the rest of the vessel, by an ancient and fishlike smell, a couple of Malays are in earnest conference: Abdrahim, the diver, and Syed, his tender. In the bronzed hand of the former lies a lustrous and beautiful pearl, a globe of soft moonlight, such a pearl as is found but twice in a century. Both men know that it is of priceless value, and are eagerly gloating over it, discussing, meanwhile, the best way of disposing of their find to the greatest possible advantage. Presently Abdrahim wraps up the treasure in a piece of rag and places it in his box, which he locks; then, followed by Syed, goes on deck, and proceeds to array himself in his diving-gear. This completed, he is helped over the side and stands on the wooden rung of the short ladder, with his head and shoulders above the surface of the water, waiting while Syed and a Kanaka put on the helmet and screw in the mouthpiece. Take your last look at the bright sunlight, and inhale your last breath of the fresh sea-breeze, Abdrahim, for that pure, flawless gem has done its work.

The helmeted head disappears beneath the unruffled surface of the sea, and Syed takes his place at the pump. The nondescript crew pay little heed to his actions; again and again the life-line quivers, but Syed is lost in a pleasant dream of the future in which he wonders at the surpassing folly of his countryman in trusting his life in his hands just after showing him the glorious pearl hidden away in the cabin. Abdrahim, he knows well, is suffocating below the lugger's keel, but the Malay's swarthy features are calm and emotionless until he suddenly calls loudly to the others, and they drag to the surface the now lifeless form of the diver. An accident, of course—something must have gone wrong with the pump, he rapidly explains to the men as they divest the corpse of the dress, and laying it on the deck, cover it with a spare sail. Towards evening a breeze springs up, and the lugger, with the dead Malay on board, steers for Thursday Island.

*   *   *

The little township on the island is fast asleep, eight bells have been struck on board the E. and A. steamer at anchor in the stream, and the last sound of revelry has died away. Near an old boatshed, in whispered conversation, stand Syed and a Chinaman. The Malay is excited and eager, the Chinaman apathetic, with a cunning assumption of indifference. The big pearl is being extolled on one side and depreciated on the other. Subtle Hi Long is assuring Syed that he has quite overestimated the worth of his find, and the Malay is vehemently asserting its wonderful value. They part, after long dispute, Hi Long calm and confident, Syed angry and upset. He coils up in his blankets under the old boatshed, and after an hour or two of troubled tossing falls into a deep slumber that lasts until long after sunrise. When he awakes he sits up, fumbles underneath the bundle that serves him for a pillow, and draws out a common red silk handkerchief with a knot tied in one corner; glancing apprehensively around, he unties the knot to feast his gaze upon his treasure. With a yell he springs up, his eyes ablaze with fury and despair, for the big pearl is gone. He has been robbed during his late sleep. A mist of blood swims before his eyes and blots out all his dreams of wealth. Blood—that is what he wants, and he draws his knife and rushes through the door out on the beach, no longer a man but a beast of prey, a Malay running amok, seeking to glut his raging thirst for vengeance on the first object crossing his path. A group of coloured men are right in his way, and almost before they are aware of it he is amongst them, striking and stabbing right and left, seeing before him nothing but a crowd of grinning Chinese, taunting him with the loss of his fortune. Two are

122

knifed before they can recover from their surprise; one of the remainder has, fortunately, an axe in his hand, and before the madman can stab again he is cut down. He rises once more with the blood streaming down his face and rushes out on the boat-jetty, leaving a ruby track on the rough stones. With one last wild stab at the phantom fleeing before him, he plunges into the sea, and Syed has gone to reckon with the ghost of the murdered Abdrahim.

The E. and A. steamer going south that morning has an additional steerage passenger in the person of Hi Long, who finds he has urgent business which compels him to leave Thursday Island immediately.

*   *   *

Through the still waters, guarded by the great barrier of coral, the steamer pursues her southern course. For two nights she has had to anchor amongst the then little known dangers of the treacherous northern coast, and now, on the third, the steady pulsation of the engines tells that she is running at half-speed through a comparatively open sea. The officer on the bridge is talking to the coast pilot as they pass backwards and forwards. Unobserved a figure rises from amongst those recumbent on the fore-hatch and approaches the side. The coloured man on watch on forward happens to turn round. 'Hoy, Chinaman!' he yells. Too late: there is a splash, and the two men on the bridge are just in time to see a white face gleam past the bar of light.

The telegraph rings and the steamer comes quickly round.

'One of the Chinese passengers just jumped overboard, sir,' says the officer to the captain when he comes on the bridge.

A boat is lowered, uselessly of course. Hi Long, after gambling away all his gains, including the big pearl stolen from Syed, has gone to the bottom.

'Why the deuce couldn't he have done it quietly?' says the captain, as the boat is being run up to the davits; 'we've lost half-an-hour through him.'

About the Author

Ernest Favenc, writer, journalist, historian and explorer, was a descendent of the Huguenots who fled religious persecution in France in the seventeenth century. Educated at Oxford and Berlin, he came to Australia in 1863, where he worked on stations in North Queensland as station hand, drover and superintendent. He also participated in the push for mineral wealth that was inspired by gold strikes in the region in the late 1860s and the 1870s. In 1878–1879 Favenc led an expedition to the previously unexplored area between Blackall and Darwin to assess the practicability of a railway link from Brisbane. His reports appeared in the *Queenslander*, where he also published poetry, stories and serials.

In 1880 he married Bessie Matthews and moved to Sydney. Favenc's residence in Sydney was interrupted in the 1880s by expeditions into the Northern Territory, where he speculated in land ownership, and into Western Australia. His services were sought after because of his acquired bushcraft skills and knowledge of the outback. Favenc put his skills to good use when he worked for the *Evening News*, and contributed fiction and poetry to the *Sydney Mail*, the *Bulletin*, the *Queensland Punch* and the *Australasian*. He also published several books.

His first major work *History of Australian Exploration 1788–1888* (1888), supported by the New South Wales government, was very successful and remains a useful reference tool. He also wrote short fiction, namely *The Last of Six: Tales of the Austral Tropics* (1893); novels, *The Secret of the Australian Desert* (1895) about the fate of the explorer Ludwig Leichhardt and *Marooned on Australia* (1896) based on the fate of the crew of the *Batavia;* and his only volume of poetry, *Voices of the Desert* (1905). His children's books mix historical fact with fantasy. Despite his close dealings with Aboriginal people, in *The Secret of the Australian Desert* (1895) he invented an alternative Indigenous race given to strange and exotic customs.

Selective Bibliography of the Published Works of Ernest Favenc

FICTION

The Secret of the Australian Desert. London: Blackie, 1895.

The Last of Six: Tales of the Austral Tropics. London: Osgood, McIlvaine, 1894.

Marooned on Australia: Being the Narration by Diedrich Buys of His Discoveries and Exploits in Terra Australis Incognita about the Year 1630. London: Blackie, 1896.

The Moccasins of Silence. Melbourne: George Robertson, 1896.

My Only Murder and Other Tales. Melbourne: George Robertson, 1899.

Tales for Young Australia. Sydney: Empson, ca.1900.

Voices of the Desert. London: Elliot Stock, 1905.

NON-FICTION

The Great Austral Plain: Its Past, Present and Future. Sydney: H.R. Woods, 1881.

The Explorers of Australia and Their Life-Work. Christchurch: Whitcombe and Tombs, 1908.

www.ingramcontent.com/pod-product-compliance
Lightning Source LLC
Chambersburg PA
CBHW060331260626
47160CB00007B/2774